Then y...

*Harlequin Blaze's bestselling miniseries
continues with more irresistible men
from all branches of the armed forces.*

Don't miss

HIS TO PROTECT
By Karen Rock
October 2016

CHRISTMAS WITH THE MARINE
By Candace Havens
November 2016

RESCUE ME
By Kira Sinclair
December 2016

Dear Reader,

The minute I read an article about Military Working Dogs I knew I had to write a story highlighting these amazing animals and the soldiers who serve beside them. It takes a special kind of person to form that bond with a highly trained K-9.

For Ty Colson, working with dogs has always been easier than dealing with people. Unlike almost everyone else in his life, no dog ever failed him. For Van Cantrell, accepting the dog injured in the same bomb blast that killed her brother is a challenge. But the more difficult obstacle is confronting the complicated man who delivers Kaia...a man she wants to hate but can't help loving.

And while it was easy for me to fall in love with Ty and Van, it was even easier to tumble head over heels for Kaia.

Military Working Dogs dedicate their lives to serving our country just like every other US soldier. But when they can no longer serve that purpose, their journey back to a normal existence and a family who can love and support them is often difficult. However, there are organizations that provide funds and programs to assist in this transition. If you're interested in learning more please visit missionk9rescue.org/about-mission-k9-rescue.

I hope you enjoy reading Ty, Van and Kaia's story! I'd love to hear from you at kirasinclair.com, or come chat with me on Twitter, @kirasinclair.

Best wishes,

Kira

Kira Sinclair

Handle Me

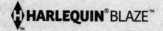
HARLEQUIN® BLAZE™

Recycling programs
for this product may
not exist in your area.

ISBN-13: 978-0-373-79911-4

Handle Me

Copyright © 2016 by Kira Bazzel

Printed in U.S.A.

www.Harlequin.com

Kira Sinclair writes emotional, passionate contemporary romances. A double winner of the National Readers' Choice Award, her first foray into writing fiction was for a high school English assignment. Nothing could dampen her enthusiasm... not even being forced to read the love story aloud to the class. Writing about sexy heroes and strong women has always excited her. She lives with her two beautiful daughters in North Alabama. Kira loves to hear from readers at kirasinclair.com.

To get the inside scoop on Harlequin Blaze and its talented writers, be sure to check out blazeauthors.com.

All backlist available in ebook format.

Visit the Author Profile page at Harlequin.com for more titles.

For all the men, women and dogs who put their lives on the line every day to protect our country, our freedom and our way of life.

1

THE MOMENT WAS HAZY. Surreal. Nothing about this day should be happening. And yet, it was.

Numbness, desperate numbness, had finally begun to spread through his body thanks to the expensive bottle of whiskey Ty Colson had brought to his best friend's wake.

Ryan would be pissed at all the somber faces and tears. They'd served together, so had talked about what they wanted if the worst actually happened.

Ty always thought it would be him.

It should have been him.

Hell, there wasn't a single soul in his life who would care if he died. At least, not now that Ryan was gone.

But his buddy... Ty's swimming, unsteady gaze dragged across the crowd of people who'd forced themselves into Ryan's parents' home. His buddy had so many people who would miss him.

An ache centered in the middle of Ty's chest. He countered the pain by pouring another shot of liquor into the glass beside him, then slammed it back.

"Is this really how you want to pay your respects to my brother?"

Savannah Cantrell's smooth, smoky voice slipped

down his spine. Another ache, a familiar one, centered much further south, kicked into overdrive.

His gaze dragged from the golden-brown liquid sloshing over the side of his glass, up the perfect black dress that hugged her body, across the pale skin of her face to eyes that were pinched, unhappy and full of judgment.

So what else was new?

Van had hated him for years. No doubt blamed him for Ryan's death, too.

She wouldn't be wrong. Not really.

"Yes, as a matter of fact it is," Ty said, happy to realize none of his words slurred. A shit-ton of whiskey might be coursing through his veins, but he'd be damned if he'd let anyone realize just how wrecked he was.

Especially Van.

"Ryan wouldn't have wanted this melancholy bullshit and you know it."

Van's mouth compressed. He expected her to start spewing a diatribe. Instead, to his utter shock, her chin began to quiver.

He hadn't seen her cry once today. And that bothered him. Not because he didn't think she was heartbroken over Ryan's death—he knew she was—but because he understood, better than anyone, that she needed the release.

Van didn't like anything messy or out of place. She liked her life perfect and controlled. He could have told her that was only an illusion, one easily killed by a single bomb blast.

Even now, her eyes glistened, but her jaw clamped tight, her will kicking in as she refused to let a single tear fall.

"Well, shit," he growled. He couldn't just let her stand there, fighting alone.

Ty reached for her, wrapping her in his arms. He offered her the only thing he had—comfort and understanding. Even as he braced for the inevitable rebuff.

Van hadn't wanted anything from him in years.

But to his surprise, Van melted into him. Her body sagged as she buried her face into the crook of his neck. Her sweet, tempting scent ballooned around him. Something soft and feminine. Expensive.

Awareness crackled across his skin. He tried to ignore it, but that was difficult. Especially when she was right there, wrapped in his arms, his better judgment dulled by half a bottle of whiskey.

They stood for several moments, silent. She didn't cry. That was a battle he'd always known she'd win. But her body trembled. The soft, almost imperceptible quiver running just beneath the surface of her skin as she fought to regain control impacted him more.

After several moments she breathed, "Get me out of here."

She didn't have to ask twice. Grabbing the neck of the bottle with one hand, Ty wrapped his other arm around her. He ushered her through the throng of people, effectively cutting off several who tried to engage her in conversations she couldn't entertain, then headed out the back door.

He was in no shape to drive and it was already dark, so their options were limited. But there was a tree house in the very back corner of the huge lot. If nothing else, it would give her some privacy and a break from the well-meaning mourners.

He and Ryan had helped Van's dad, Nick, build the

tree house when they were younger. Ty remembered the heat, the pain of smashing his thumb with a hammer and the sense of pride when they'd all stood together after weeks of work to admire the finished product. One of Nick's arms had been slung around Ty's shoulders, the other around Ryan's. In that moment, he'd felt like he belonged.

From the ground, Ty watched Van climb up the pieces of wood nailed crookedly to the trunk of the huge tree. More memories flashed through his mind. Van, her dark brown hair in a single long braid, twisting around and sticking her tongue out at him. She'd tattled to her mom because he and Ryan wouldn't let her up. Margaret had come out and given them both a lecture about how they should treat little girls.

But now, he broke every one of those rules as Van's skirt belled out from her legs, flashing a glimpse of round curves and pale skin covered in black lace panties. A gentleman would have looked away; Ty couldn't claim that title, no matter how many lectures Margaret had given.

His body responded with purpose at the tantalizing view. No whiskey dick for him.

This wasn't a good idea.

Ty thought about turning around and heading back into the house when Van tipped backward and looked over her shoulder. "You coming or what?"

There was something taunting about her tone. Something that spurred him into action.

Grasping a rough-hewn board, Ty hauled himself up the tree and through the entrance they'd cut in the floor so many years ago.

The memories of building this place were some of the best of his childhood. At the moment, they were also some of the worst. Knowing his friend could never come up here again hurt like hell.

Here, the past assaulted him more than anywhere else, weighing him down with regret. Until his unsteady gaze drifted around, finally landing on Savannah.

The past and the present merged. Maybe it was the alcohol, or the day, or his grief. But he could see the child she'd been lurking inside the strong, stubborn, successful woman she'd become.

Savannah Cantrell was the girl he'd always wanted. The woman he could never have.

Van reached out and grabbed the bottle of whiskey from him. He hadn't remembered he'd tucked it under his arm. She lifted it to her deep pink lips and took a big gulp.

She sputtered, grimaced, sucked in air, then did it again.

"Easy, princess." Ty moved for the bottle, but she pulled it out of his reach.

"I need to catch up."

"You need to slow down or you're going to end the night with your head hanging over the toilet."

Savannah stared at him for several seconds, her expression blank. Then she tipped her head back and laughed. Belly-clutching, rolling laughter that was so out of place it felt ragged and painful.

All Ty could do was growl at her, "What the heck is so funny?"

"Do you know I've never gotten so drunk that I puked?"

"I'm pretty sure that's a good thing."

"I'm thirty-two years old, Ty, and I've never been really drunk. I've never had a one-night stand. Hell, I can count on one hand the number of men I've slept with. And I promise you most of them weren't worth the effort."

What the hell was he supposed to say to that?

"I've spent my entire life doing the right thing. Making the right—safe—decisions. Working hard. Hell, I save lives for a living. But what goddamn good is that when Ryan is dead?"

Van grimaced and tipped the bottle back again. Ty wanted to wipe away the grief that sharpened her words and dulled her gorgeous eyes. But he couldn't.

"So, tonight I'm going to get knee-walking drunk. I'm entitled. Feel free to go if you don't want to watch the show."

There was no way in hell he was leaving her alone. Not like this.

"For God's sake, at least tell me you've eaten something today."

Her lips twisted into a bastardized version of her smooth smile. "Nope. At least nothing that counts."

She was going to hurt in the morning. But then, she was going to hurt tomorrow no matter what she did tonight. Ty understood the desire to drown the pain in alcohol at least for a little while. Wasn't that what he'd been doing not thirty minutes ago?

"Fine, but you can't drink alone."

"Whatever."

A breeze swirled through the open square windows. A shiver racked Van's body. Ty could see the goose bumps spreading across her naked shoulders and arms from across the tree house.

Shaking his head, Ty walked over to the large plastic bin sitting on the far side of the small space. Lifting the lid, he found several old quilts and a couple of worn throw pillows Margaret had donated to the cause years ago when she'd remodeled.

They smelled of dust and age, but were dry and clean thanks to the well-sealed bin. Dragging them out, he spread one blanket across the floor, threw the pillows against the bin for support and left the second blanket in a pile so Van could wrap up. It might be early spring in Texas, but the nights could still feel like winter.

"Sit."

Ty could tell the whiskey was already hitting her. Steady, perfect Van tottered as she tried to lower her body gracefully to the ground.

Instinct had him reaching for her, but she shoved his helpful hands away.

With a sigh, he settled beside her. Almost shoulder to shoulder, but Ty made sure not to touch her. Not just because it was obvious she didn't want him to, but because he wasn't really interested in torturing himself any more than necessary.

They sat in silence for a while, passing the bottle back and forth. She didn't seem to notice that he barely took a sip when it was his turn. Or maybe she did and didn't particularly care. Either way, the heavy silence didn't last.

After about fifteen minutes Van broke it. "Do you remember that time you and Ryan crashed my slumber party?"

Of course he remembered. That was the night he finally realized Van was no longer the little sister who'd followed blindly behind his best friend, but a young woman with breasts and hips and soft pink lips he suddenly wanted to crush beneath his own.

He could have stopped her from sharing more—should have—but he didn't.

He needed the good memories right now, because the bad ones felt like they were going to crush him.

A laugh fell from her parted lips, not quite bright, but not quite broken. "God, I was so pissed at y'all. I'd worked hard to get Kelley Morgan and Julia Price to come over. You guys scared the shit out of us and they both went screaming home in the middle of the night. Ruined my fifteenth birthday."

That wasn't the way he remembered it. "We didn't ruin a damn thing. Kelley had a thing for Ryan and was only there because she thought you were her ticket into his pants. We were doing you a favor."

Van shoved his shoulder, pushing him sideways. "You don't think I knew that? Hell, I promised they could bump into him in the hallway after his shower, wearing nothing but a towel."

Ty slowly turned to face her. "You pimped out your own brother just to get those girls to come to your birthday party?"

She shrugged. "What can I say? Not my finest moment. And you can't convince me Ryan would have cared."

No. No he wouldn't have.

Shaking his head, Ty said, "God, I've missed you." He had no intention of saying the words aloud, but apparently the whiskey had lubricated his tongue.

She grinned, her gorgeous pink mouth going wide and a little lopsided. Her gaze was blurry and bright, her movements sluggish as her shoulder bumped his and her head rested against him. "Me, too. Sucks, you know?"

She swayed slightly. Ty wrapped an arm around her waist, pulling her against him to stabilize her. He stared down at her, a jumble of emotions tangling inside. Maybe if he'd been sober he could have sorted them out, but right now, that ability was lost to him.

What he did know was that she was beautiful and in his arms. Exactly where he'd always wanted her, but never expected her to be.

If she'd kept that aloof edge she used as a buffer he might have been able to resist. But her expression changed. The laughter melted away to something deeper, darker. Something he recognized because he felt it, too.

Need.

God, he couldn't be good when she was looking at him that way.

Without thinking about it, Ty leaned down and kissed her, something he'd wanted since that summer she'd turned fifteen.

He couldn't have her back then.

Hell, he couldn't really have her now.

But the way she responded to him…he couldn't let her go, either. Not tonight.

She made a sound deep in her throat, a strangled cry mixed with a whimper. The echo of it shot straight to his cock, as her fingers clenched in his shirt, wrinkling the fabric. But he didn't give a shit. Because she wasn't pushing him away, she was tugging him closer.

Her head fell back, offering her mouth, opening to give him more.

He couldn't remember how it happened, but one minute they were sitting next to each other, the next Van was stretched out on the floor, the length of his body pressed tight against hers.

His hands trembled as they raced over her curves. He tried to memorize every sound, every reaction, before something could take them away again.

He wasn't built for nice. Didn't deserve beautiful. And Van was both of those things.

She arched into his touch anyway, silently begging for more.

Her pale green eyes flashed, tempting him as she watched his every move.

He shouldn't be doing this. Wanting her was wrong before, and it was wrong now. Even more so, because the whiskey was clouding her judgment. And his for that matter.

He tried to pull away, to put some distance between them, but Van's grip wouldn't let go.

"Don't," she whispered, the word low and fierce.

"Don't what?"

"Don't you dare stop, Ty Colson."

Tangling their fingers together, she closed his fist around the hem of her dress and tugged upward.

He could fight himself, maybe. But he couldn't fight her. He'd never been able to deny Van anything.

If she wanted this—needed him tonight—then he'd give it to her. And deal with the inevitable fallout later.

Ty dragged her dress up her creamy thighs, over her hips and then off over her head. Her bra matched the black lace panties he'd glimpsed earlier. Of course they did. Everything about Savannah Cantrell was sophisticated and put-together.

"God, Van, do you have any idea how gorgeous you are? The men in this town must be complete idiots."

She laughed, a brief burst that was gone before it was really there. "I'm too busy for the men in this town."

Ty shook his head. "That wouldn't stop me, if I was around."

Reaching down, Ty flicked open the front clasp of

her bra, letting her generous breasts spill out. He didn't wait, leaning in to suck one deep into his mouth. She whimpered, arching into his caress. Her fingers scraped against his scalp, grasping his hair, holding him right where she wanted.

He liked that about Van. When she wanted something, she didn't hesitate to take it.

But he was used to being the alpha in any pack. Ringing her wrists with his fingers, he pulled her hands away, then wrapped them around the handle on the storage bin behind her head.

"Hold on, princess."

If this was the only time he was going to have Van Cantrell, he was going to make it memorable…for them both.

He spent the next twenty minutes torturing her, not to mention himself. His mouth and hands touched every inch of her body. Her skin was so soft and smooth, fragrant with the understated scent of her perfume and the heady fragrance of her arousal.

When he finally slipped down between her open thighs her skin was flushed and her hips writhed. Her sex glistened with need. And he was hungry to oblige.

He nibbled and teased, swirling his tongue close to her entrance before slipping up to lightly brush across her clit.

"Please, Ty. Please," Van nearly sobbed. He relished in knowing he could make her beg. Make her forget.

His tongue speared deep inside as his finger found the tight knot of her clit. It barely took anything for her to shoot off.

She clenched around him. Her thighs clamped against his ears. He expected a scream, but her mouth opened on a silent cry as her eyes screwed tight. Her entire body shook with the force of her orgasm.

Satisfaction filled him, even as his dick throbbed painfully behind his zipper. God, he'd never been so turned on in his life.

Reaching into the pocket of his pants, Ty pulled out his wallet and the condom he always had stashed there. It'd been in there for months; he seriously hoped the thing was still good.

Dropping his pants to the floor, he ripped open the packet and rolled on the condom.

Standing above her, he looked down at Van, legs spread wide on the floor at his feet. Her body seemed boneless. He'd done that to her.

She watched him with half-lidded eyes, her gaze eating him up in a way that made him want to give her a repeat performance. But he knew he couldn't survive another round, not right now, not without losing his mind.

Dropping to his knees, he reached for her, positioning the tip of his cock at her hot, wet entrance.

He waited for her to change her mind, or tell him to fuck off, but she didn't. Instead, she reached for him. Her hands cupped his ass and pulled him closer, her hips bucking and eager.

She opened her thighs wider, silently inviting him to take whatever he wanted.

God, he wanted it all. Not just now. He wanted anything he could get forever. Pain lanced through his chest, but Ty beat it back. He knew there was nothing more than tonight.

Hell, this could very well be the last time he ever saw her.

That thought sent him into a frenzy. The need to leave

his mark on her in some way was so overwhelming he couldn't logic it away.

His hips slammed against hers, claiming her in one quick, deep thrust.

Van gasped, her lips parting as her head tipped back. Her fingers dug into his ass, urging him to give her more.

"God, you feel so good, Van. Unbelievable." Ty dropped his forehead against hers. His lips brushed across her temple. Hers found his throat. She kissed him, the soft touch blending into something more when her teeth nipped at his skin.

She sucked, drawing his pounding pulse into her mouth. She was going to leave a mark of her own, but Ty didn't give a damn.

His hips pistoned against hers in deep, smooth strokes that made the world gray around them. The only thing that felt real was him and her. Together. Finally.

Her labored breaths puffed against his skin, and her mouth found him, licking and leaving rows of tiny teeth marks across his shoulders, throat and collarbone. Each tug sent a jolt straight to his cock.

She was right there with him, meeting him stroke for stroke. He could feel the walls of her sex tightening around him, so close. Ty held on, delaying his own release, which threatened to blind him.

Van whispered mindless, garbled words, but his body recognized exactly what she was asking for.

Reaching between them, Ty found her clit and thrust deep, filling her as he stroked the swollen bundle of nerves.

Her body exploded. This time his name echoed off the wooden walls around them. A surge of satisfaction pounded through him as she clamped down around him. It was more than he could take.

Burying his face in her throat, Ty allowed his release, holding tight to her as a storm raged through him. He thrust hard, drawing out the pleasure as long as he could, selfishly savoring every last drop.

Collapsing to the floor, Ty didn't notice they were lying on plywood covered with a blanket. He didn't care that he could hear the faint sounds of people leaving the house, car engines firing.

The only thing that mattered was Van in his arms. He tangled their legs together, tucked her head against his chest and grabbed the other blanket, wrapping it around them.

She didn't protest. Instead, she curled into him, letting her body melt against his.

Happiness and pain mixed together in his chest. The story of his life. Nothing good ever happened without being accompanied by a kick in the gut.

Van was silent, but not distant. She didn't pull away. Tonight, he'd take small favors wherever he could get them.

His hand stroked the soft fall of her hair, tangling in the strands as they slipped between his fingers.

"I should probably go back inside, be there to say goodbye to everyone."

He could tell by her tone that she didn't really want to. And he didn't blame her. All day he'd wanted nothing more than to run away from this place…at least, until an hour ago.

"Why bother?"

"Because my parents need me there. Because it's what I should do."

"Says who?"

"Every etiquette manual in existence."

"No one would blame you for disappearing. No one will fault you for needing an escape."

"But I shouldn't. It wouldn't be right."

Ty shifted, tipping her head back so he could look into her eyes. "No one expects you to do the right thing all the time."

"I expect it."

He shook his head. "You've always put too much pressure on yourself. Just once, let yourself do something unexpected."

Her mouth quirked up on one side, not quite a smile. "Pretty sure that's what we just did."

Her gaze slipped away from his, focusing on something over his shoulder. He wanted to draw her back. Every instinct inside him yelled that if he wanted anything further this was the moment to push.

But he couldn't.

As much as it hurt, Ty knew exactly what tonight had been. It wasn't like he didn't have plenty of experience carrying around pain, hiding it so no one else could see.

Shifting to get more comfortable, Ty tightened his hold on her. "Go to sleep. In the morning you can blame me for your disappearance. Everyone will believe I was drunk off my ass—" like mother, like son "—and you had to pour me into bed."

Her body stiffened, but after a few seconds she relaxed, a sigh slipping through her parted lips.

It didn't take five minutes for her breathing to even out and her body to go limp against his. The floor felt hard against his back, but it wasn't the first time he'd slept on something uncomfortable.

Ty's arms tightened around Van. He tipped his head back, found the sky through the window in the wall beside them and squeezed his eyes shut.

Just one more thing you're going to have to forgive me for, buddy. But, I'm going to be honest—I don't regret a damn moment.

SAVANNAH GROANED. Her entire body hurt. Her brain felt fuzzy and slow. God, would she never learn that sleeping on the tiny cots in the hospital's on-call room was a bad idea?

Shifting, her hand grazed something cold and plastic. A groan rolled through her chest as memory slammed home. She wasn't at the hospital. This pain was all self-inflicted. Though it was fuzzy, she could remember knocking back whiskey from a bottle she'd swiped from Ty.

Van's eyes popped open.

Ty.

Oh, shit.

Van rolled onto her side and pushed against the hard plywood floor. Her stomach bubbled unhappily. The walls around her wavered.

But a creaking sound filtered through her misery.

For the first time, she realized she was alone. And she hadn't fallen asleep that way.

The sky was mostly gray through the large window, with fingers of pink and orange just starting to streak across. Van crawled over and used the ledge to lever herself up—just in time to see Ty, his shirt hanging from the pocket of his slacks, shoes dangling from his fingers, sneaking across her parents' lawn toward the back gate.

She should be grateful he was walking away so she wouldn't have to face him.

But she wasn't.

Hurt, anger and indignation slammed through her, causing her sick stomach to roil even more.

God, she would never drink again.

Part of her wanted to go after him. To yell at him, for leaving, for making her feel amazing last night, for dragging her brother into a situation that had ended up killing him. For letting her get drunk and then taking advantage of her.

She wanted to blame Ty Colson for every single thing that was wrong with her life.

But she couldn't.

Last night, she might have been drunk and reckless, but Ty hadn't pushed. He hadn't done anything she didn't want. As much as she wanted to paint the man as an asshole, she knew him well enough to realize that if she'd said no at any point, he would have stopped.

Instead, she'd begged him for more.

Oh, God. Van sank back down onto her haunches and dropped her head between her knees. Sucking huge gulps of air through her nose, she willed her stomach to settle.

She would not throw up. She would not throw up.

This was better.

Ty had given her something last night that she'd desperately needed. Solace, laughter, release. A chance to forget, even if only for a few moments.

The fact that she'd never felt so whole and connected with anyone else was something she'd simply have to deal with. And get over.

On the bright side, she could mark one-night stand off her bucket list. And with the boy she'd had a teenage crush on. Oh, look, a twofer.

In the quiet silence, she could hear the engine on Ty's

rental turn over. The sound of his tires crunching across pavement, picking up speed as he fled from her neighborhood. From her life.

It hurt. Not that she'd necessarily wanted to wake up with his strong arms cradling her close. That would have been infinitely more awkward than sitting there alone in her misery and embarrassment.

This way, she didn't have to confront what she'd actually done. It was a little late in life for her to be adding stupid experiences to her resume, but maybe better late than never.

Besides, with Ryan gone, she'd likely never see Ty Colson again.

And that was the way she wanted it.

Really, it was.

2

Four months later

TY STARED AT the perfect house in front of him. Exactly
the kind of place he'd expect Van Cantrell to own.

The street was quiet, a subdued neighborhood full of
older homes. The kind with gentle laughter, sunny yel-
low walls and a kitchen with a mom making waffles and
chocolate chip cookies.

The kind of home he'd never had.

The kind of life he'd never realized was possible until
he'd met Ryan in the second grade. And learned that
sporting bruises and going to bed with a rumbling belly
weren't normal.

The neighborhood seemed sluggish. Ty missed the
normal weekday rush of people leaving for work. The
kids who would likely be running up and down the
cracked sidewalks in a few hours were still snuggled
under their sheets, dreaming of lazy summer mornings
and the remaining weeks with no homework.

Two weatherworn rocking chairs sat on the wrap-
around front porch, swaying in the hot Texas breeze.
Just waiting for someone with a steaming mug of coffee
to curl up against the wooden slats and enjoy what little

respite the morning offered before summer's oppressive heat seeped in.

A memory burst through, one he'd been pushing back for months.

Van, sitting in that exact spot, her feet pulled up underneath her. Body slumped, shoulders rounded with grief. A beautiful, golden sunrise gilding her exhausted, tear-stained face.

He'd sat there in a different car, on a different day, and been a voyeur to her pain. He'd wanted to comfort her then. But he'd fought the urge to go to her, wrap her in his arms and wipe each of her tears away.

Because he'd known it was better that way. For both of them. After the night they'd shared together in that tree house…

In that moment, being close to her and seeing the anger and accusation in her eyes again would have destroyed him.

Now silence settled over him, harsh and heavy, pressing tight against his chest. He should get out of the SUV he'd rented at the San Antonio airport—get this over with—but he couldn't seem to make his body move.

This was the moment he'd been dreading for the last several weeks. But it was as inevitable as it was filled with regret, and guilt, and a grief so bone-deep he couldn't begin to exorcise it.

The only way he'd gotten through that last trip home was by numbing himself with whiskey…and Van.

Ty's stomach churned and his hands, still wrapped around the leather-covered steering wheel, went white with tension. Sweat that had nothing to do with the heat trickled down the back of his neck.

God, he didn't want to walk inside. Didn't want to look into her gorgeous, pain-filled eyes.

There was no way to fix what was broken—for either of them.

But that didn't stop him from wishing he could roll back time and change everything. He'd give anything—absolutely anything—to bring Ryan back.

A soft whimper sounded from the backseat and a cold, wet nose nudged against his shoulder. Ty pulled a sudden gulp of air into his lungs, grateful for the jolt, which prevented him from spiraling into a familiar mental tailspin.

The last thing he needed was for Van to find him stalling in her driveway. She knew he was coming this morning. Hell, he hadn't even bothered to check into his hotel first. Better to get this over with.

Carefully unwrapping his fingers from the wheel, Ty reached back and scratched behind Kaia's ears. She let out another sound, only this time it was full of pleasure. Leaning her head against Ty's shoulder, she angled her body for a deeper rub.

"I know, girl," he whispered. "You're almost home. It's almost over."

At least he could make things better for her. Kaia had been through as much trauma and grief as he had. As Savannah had.

He was really hoping that Kaia's presence would give Van some small measure of comfort. He knew the dog desperately needed some love and affection. He'd fought for months to bring her home because he knew it was what Ryan would have wanted.

Kaia let out a short, sharp bark.

Pushing out a gush of air, Ty tried to laugh. The sound

was off, rusty and forced. "I guess it's time to get this over with."

Forcefully pulling his gaze from the house, Ty climbed from the car. He opened the back door wide and gave the command for Kaia to jump down. He didn't bother with a leash. A Belgian Malinois, she'd been trained as an SSD, a specialized search dog, and had spent the better part of five years scenting for explosives and bombs, primarily following voice commands. She was extremely intelligent and very obedient. All of their dogs were.

It was hard not to be partial to his own partner, Echo, waiting for him back in Afghanistan, but he was just as comfortable with Kaia.

The dog's long, lithe body stretched forward, then didn't hesitate, bounding from the SUV, and landing on the ground with a stuttered gait. The loss of her left front leg barely even slowed her down.

But Ty remembered. The sight of Ryan's soot-covered, broken body in the rubble. Kaia, her fur matted with blood—Ryan's and hers—lying over him. Protecting him. Unwilling to move even as a burning fire raged just feet away, her hair smoking from the heat.

Ty recalled the pain and sadness that had filled her eyes when he had finally reached them, pulling his best friend and the dog who'd tried to protect him to cover— it had been too late to save Ryan. And Kaia had almost lost her life as well.

Weeks of surgery and therapy. Months of waiting for her to be medically cleared, released from service and then pronounced adoptable before he'd been able to even make the argument she should be sent home to Ryan's family. A trip that he'd paid for out of his own pocket since the military didn't cover the expense of transporting retired dogs to their new homes.

Worth every goddamn penny. It was the least he owed his best friend.

Ordering Kaia to heel with a simple hand gesture, Ty turned from the car, but then stopped a step away. The dog followed his lead, even without a command, pressing her shoulder against his thigh to compensate for the loss of her limb.

The porch was no longer empty. Van stood there, arms crossed over her chest, watching him. Watching them both.

Her expression was…unreadable. Distant and closed. But that wasn't unusual when he was around. Did she remember the last time they'd seen each other? Or had she been so affected by the alcohol and grief that the memories had disappeared?

Those memories, the way her body had felt against his. The scent of her skin. The tangy, tempting taste of her mouth… He remembered every second.

But, even if she did remember, he fully expected Van to pretend she didn't. Because they both knew that single night was a…well, *mistake* was the wrong word because it implied he hadn't wanted it to happen, which definitely wasn't true. That night had been a fantasy, even as he'd known Van was grieving and wanted nothing more than a physical release from the pressure of her loss.

It was clear from her expression that the remote, disapproving woman he'd grown to expect was back today. Van hadn't always been that way with him. There'd been a time when he'd considered her as much a friend as Ryan. But it had been a long while since that was true.

Her skin was still creamy pale. Her hair, loose and

blowing in the soft morning breeze, a rich, dark brown that bordered on black. Her eyes were a pale green and he knew, up close, they had flecks of golden brown shot through them.

But it was the tilt of her chin that always got him. The cool, calm bravado she approached everything with. Competence and confidence. Van's philosophy was very much to fake it till you make it.

Nothing ruffled her feathers, least of all him.

A stinging pain lanced through his chest. Ty stopped himself from reaching up to rub at it, the motion a pointless reflex. He knew by now that nothing would take it away.

He took a step forward. Kaia lurched up, hop-stepping in time with his movements, staying perfectly even with his hip as he moved to close the gap between them.

Something sharp flashed through Van's gaze as she watched the dog's halting progress. Her body swayed as they reached the front steps, as if she wanted to reach out. Help.

But she didn't.

Ty didn't stop at the bottom. He didn't even pause at the top. He kept moving until he could feel the heat drifting from her body. Leaning down into her personal space, he pressed his lips to her temple. Her body stiffened. He wasn't touching her anywhere else, but he could still feel it. Her tension radiated out like a magnet flipped to its opposing pole, trying to push him away.

"It's good to see you, Van."

She didn't respond. Didn't have to. He knew she didn't agree.

Pulling away from him, her gaze skittered over his face for several seconds, then down his body, tracing each arm, his torso, legs and feet, until it came to rest at the dog sitting patiently beside him.

"Kaia?" she finally asked in her soft, smooth voice, the one that always sent a wave of longing washing over him. Today was no different.

Ty nodded, placing a hand on the furred head at his hip, scratching behind her ears.

Van slowly sank in front of him. She didn't reach out to the dog. Instead, she wrapped her arms around her own folded legs, hugging her body into a tight ball. The two stared at each other for several seconds, neither of them moving.

Finally, she extended a hand. Her fingers trembled. If he hadn't been watching he might not have noticed the tiny crack in her smooth exterior. Van was good at bottling her emotions. Until she wasn't, and then the explosion...

He'd experienced her anger and passion on several occasions. It was a sight to behold.

Her wide mouth tugged down at the corners, the hint of a frown.

"I'm so sorry," she breathed out, her fingers slipping hesitantly over the spot where the vet had sewn up Kaia's leg. The dog didn't flinch or move, just sat quietly.

Van's hand drifted upward, coming to rest on the fuzzy head. She looked straight into Kaia's watchful gaze and whispered, "Thank you."

Ty fought against the lump forming in his throat. He wanted to look away, but the motion of Van standing up pulled his attention back.

This time her gaze flicked over him quickly, there and away. She turned her back to him, tossing words over her shoulder. "I guess you should come in."

Van didn't want him there. Didn't want him in her home.

She didn't bother to look back to see if he was following her inside. She didn't have to. She knew.

Where Ty Colson was concerned, she had a sixth sense and always had. Growing up, he'd been a fixture in her family. Ryan had been his shadow, following his lead into whatever trouble the wild boy could dream up.

And, oh, Ty could dream up a shit-ton of trouble.

She'd been the annoying little sister relentlessly tagging along. The high-pitched voice of reason always cautioning that they were going to get caught and punished. Quick to say, "I told you so," when her predictions came true.

But somewhere along the way, her childish fascination with him morphed into something more. An adolescent crush that made her feel awkward around the boy she'd known most of her life.

To her, Ty Colson was perfect. Adventurous. Wild and uninhibited. Remote to almost everyone…except her. There were times she'd envied the freedom he always had, even as she realized it meant no one at home cared enough to rein him in. She'd seen his wounds and wanted nothing more than to soothe them.

Until his antics got both boys in real trouble and sent her brother's life careening off course.

Her simple, innocent attraction to him had gotten muddled up with resentment and blame. Not that those emotions had stemmed the physical awareness.

So damn frustrating.

Even now, Van could feel him, walking several paces behind her. She could sense the motion of his body as he tempered his gait to match the wounded dog at his side.

She couldn't seem to turn off the relief she'd felt when

he'd first walked up, her gaze devouring him, searching for signs of wear and injury. There'd been a pressure in her chest until she could see for herself that he was okay. Even as her brain told her she shouldn't care.

God, what was wrong with her? Ty had gotten her brother killed. Maybe not directly, but he was responsible. Ryan never should have been in Afghanistan. Never should have become a dog handler, searching the unforgiving terrain for explosive devices just waiting to maim and kill.

Van walked straight back to the kitchen, which looked out onto the yard. When she was growing up, her family had always gathered in the kitchen. Now, in her own home, the kitchen gave her peace—it was the place she came to when she needed a break from the storm her life could be.

It was the only place where she felt like she could breathe deeply.

Out of the corner of her eye, she registered Ty standing in the middle of her doorway. Just there, watching, waiting. For what, she wasn't sure. And that left her restless.

Needing something to do, Van lifted the mug of coffee she'd left on the counter when she'd heard Ty drive up and took a sip, making a face when she realized it had gone cold.

Nothing worse than cold coffee.

Dumping it out, she popped another pod into the machine, pushed the button and let it run.

This day was going to require copious amounts of caffeine.

Not only was she an emotional wreck, but she'd just gotten off back-to-back shifts at the hospital. They'd had a late-night trauma call, gunshot to the abdomen. The guy had coded on her table twice before finally stabilizing enough for them to transport him to surgery.

Even now, she had no idea if he'd made it or not. One of the downfalls of ER medicine. She patched them up, sent them either out the door or on to someone else and then rarely knew what happened next.

But the rush of saving someone's life...worth every second of exhaustion.

While her coffee was brewing, Van reached into a cupboard and pulled down a bright turquoise Fiesta bowl. She filled it with water and placed it on the floor near the sink.

"Do you have food for her?" she asked.

There was no point in pleasantries with the man who'd sauntered closer and was now leaning against the edge of her kitchen island. Way too much history between them to bother.

"In the car. I'll get it in a bit."

The low timbre of his voice slipped across her skin, giving her goose bumps. He might as well have touched her, given the effect he had.

Dammit.

Clenching her teeth, Van turned. Better to get this over with.

"How long will you be in town?"

There was a part of her that didn't want to ask. Didn't want to know when he'd be returning to the same dangerous place that had taken her brother. But the rest of her needed to know just how long she'd have to deal with the tension stringing her body so tight she was afraid she might snap.

"I've got two weeks. I figured I'd stay here for a bit.

The town council asked me to ride with Kaia as marshal in the Fourth of July parade."

Great. They'd asked her to as well. Not that she'd expected to avoid him the entire time, but she was hoping to minimize their interaction.

Van just nodded, keeping the information that she'd be there, too, to herself. Maybe she could find a way out of it. If he was there, what did they need her for?

It was bad enough that they were going to be honoring Ryan. She wasn't sure she could deal with the pain of it all again. Losing him was still too raw.

"I'll see how you and Kaia are coming along with your training. If you guys are good then I might head to a beach somewhere for a few days before I go back."

"Training?"

A frown creased the spot right between his blue-gray eyes. She'd always been fascinated with them. The color was so…unusual. And it changed depending on what he wore or what mood he was in.

When she was younger, she used to make up excuses to loiter in the same room as the boys, pretending to read a book or watch a movie. In reality, she'd observed him. Noticed how he guarded himself with everyone—except her family.

As a teenager, she'd watched him go through girls, and fought against the jealousy she couldn't quite conquer. He'd take them out. Treat them like queens. But never really give them anything of himself. No girl lasted more than a few weeks.

In high school, he'd gotten a reputation for being aloof, but stellar in bed. Details she really hadn't wanted to know—because it only made her fantasies about him worse—but couldn't quite escape. Van had gotten sick of being the go-to girl for information and advice on how to catch him. Everyone seemed to think she held the code.

And maybe she did. She had to admit, it'd felt amazing to have him come up to her during a football game, sling his arm around her shoulder and include her in whatever conversation he had going.

As far as she knew, he'd never had a long-term relationship. Not that his career really offered the opportunity to find love.

That was a laugh. Because neither did hers. Eight years of college and medical school, four years of residency. Long hours in the ER and plenty of stress. She'd tried dating in her mid-twenties. Had a solid relationship that lasted about eight months.

Ty shifted, his hips sliding against the counter behind him. God, he looked good. But, then, he always had. His biceps bulged against the tight sleeves of the faded T-shirt he'd thrown on this morning. Ink snaked down his right arm, stark black against the golden tan of his skin.

His thighs were huge. She'd bet she couldn't wrap both hands around the circumference of one. She'd kill to see him in a pair of running shorts, the ropy muscles bunching and straining with movement. She was definitely a leg and ass girl.

"I had to sign an agreement, on your behalf."

It took Van several seconds to realize what Ty was talking about. Oh, yeah, they were discussing the dog… and not Ty Colson's fine physique.

"Kaia can no longer be used for security or patrolling, but she knows plenty of commands, most of them you shouldn't need. Since I'm here, I wanted to teach you the few that would be useful."

Van's eyes went wide. Honestly, when her parents had

first told her Ty had contacted them about adopting Kaia she hadn't known how to feel. Conflicted was really the only choice.

She'd heard Ty tell friends and family at the funeral about how Kaia had stayed with Ryan at the end, draping her body over his in a valiant attempt to shield him, despite her own injuries. She was a soldier, willing to die, and deserved to be rewarded for her service.

But every time Van's gaze met Kaia's, taking in her dark brown, watchful eyes and missing leg, a blast of grief shot through her chest. The dog was going to be a constant reminder of Ryan's death. One she wasn't sure she was strong enough to endure.

She'd actually been talking about getting a dog for months. She was out of her residency and established in her new career. Tired of coming home to an empty house. She'd mentioned it to her parents, knowing she'd need their help on the days she worked long shifts.

She'd been ready to pull the trigger, but her plans had been put on hold when they'd received word that Ryan had died. And since then it just hadn't felt right.

But now, how could she say no to taking Kaia? Just thinking about it had made her feel guilty as hell.

Although, if she'd known agreeing would include training sessions with Ty, she probably would have worked harder to find a reason to refuse.

If looking at Kaia had her conflicted, looking at Ty was so much worse.

She hated him. She cared about him. She wanted to hurt him the way she was hurting. She wanted to make sure he was okay.

Honestly, she had no idea what to do with the man and

the jumble of emotions he made her feel. It was so much easier just not to deal with them…or him.

But that plan wasn't going to work for the next couple weeks.

Shit.

"Fine. I took a couple weeks off work to get Kaia settled. I'm sure we can find some time to go over things. Why don't you give me a call after you've checked into your hotel and we can set something up for tomorrow." Might as well get this over with.

Ty nodded, a soft curl of dirty-blond hair flopping over into his eye. Her fingers tingled with the need to reach over and push it out of the way. Instead, she tightened her grip on the counter.

Silence pressed in on the moment, uncomfortably filling the space between them.

Words she didn't want to say crawled up the back of her throat. But she swallowed them down. They wouldn't change anything. Wouldn't bring her brother back. Couldn't purge the anger and grief, frustration and accusation. Or the unwanted desire and hot memories that had been haunting her dreams for the past four months.

So, as always, she stayed quiet, bottling it inside until the emotions were one big swirl of confusing sludge sucking at the center of her chest.

After several minutes, Ty said, "I'll go get Kaia's things," and turned to walk away.

Van heard the front door open and close. Kaia's ears pricked, but she didn't move from her sentry position beside the doorway.

God, it was going to be a very long two weeks.

3

"AGAIN."

Ty watched frustration pinch Van's mouth. Given any other set of circumstances, the expression might have been endearing. It wasn't often that Savannah Cantrell struggled with anything. She was a brilliant ER doctor and one of the most intelligent women Ty had ever met.

She'd always been better, smarter than he was. Hell, too wrapped up in his own anger and shitty life, he'd barely graduated high school.

The problem was, she wasn't the only one suffering.

Kaia, already struggling to compensate for her missing limb, was desperate to prove herself to her new owner. But Van kept giving the poor dog mixed signals. Kaia wasn't sure what Van wanted…mostly because Van didn't seem to have a clue what she wanted the dog to do, either.

Van's bangs flopped against her forehead as she blew a stream of frustrated air from her mouth.

"Let's be honest, Ty, I don't think doing it again is going to help." He watched her expression, now wary and guarded, flit over Kaia. "Maybe taking her isn't such a good idea."

Nope. He had to shut that train of thought down.

Stalking across Van's sunny backyard, he stopped several feet from Kaia. Gaining her attention, Ty lowered his voice and issued a single command. "Heel."

Kaia immediately obeyed. Her ears perked up and her body practically vibrated as she moved into the correct position.

"Watch her body language. She wants to obey. She needs you to assume the role of alpha and tell her what to do. Kaia lives to please. Some dogs respond to food or toys. This one laps up praise. It's part of the reason she and Ryan had such a close bond."

Van shook her head. "I don't know that I can do this."

"Yes, you can. You can't stand there and tell me you treat the staff in your ER with kid gloves."

"Of course not. We're all professionals and we have a job to do."

Ty nodded. "So does Kaia. Her job is to obey your commands. If you walked into the ER while a patient was coding and whispered, what would happen?"

Van crossed her arms over her chest. "Nothing."

"Exactly. Everyone would be too busy, upset or lost in their own thoughts to pay attention. Kaia is the same way. She's a highly trained animal. She's constantly evaluating her surroundings, which can be a good thing. But not when you want her attention. You have to be louder, stronger and more authoritative than anything else—including her instincts. So, try again."

Van pulled a huge breath in. She held it for several seconds before letting it go.

A few moments earlier, her body language had been frustrated and unsure. Now she was in control—of herself and hopefully Kaia.

"Kaia, heel."

This time, Van's voice was low and strong, holding the bite of authority.

Kaia rolled her eyes up at him, but Ty sat unmoving. Reinforcing the command Van had just given would countermand everything they were trying to accomplish. Van needed to find her voice and Kaia needed to recognize her as the new authority in her life.

After a moment of hesitation, Kaia limped over to Van's side. She sat on her haunches, nudging her nose against the fist Van had clenched near her thigh.

"Praise her," Ty murmured.

"Good girl, Kaia," Van nearly whispered.

"You can do better than that. Kaia craves affection. Give her what she wants when she does something right."

Van held back for several seconds before turning to the dog and lavishing her with attention. The difference in both the woman and the animal was astonishing. The minute Van's hands surrounded Kaia's face, rubbing against her soft fur and giving sweet words, both of them began to shine.

For a brief moment, he wondered what it would take for him to get that kind of affection from Van again.

What a stupid thought since he already knew the answer—generous amounts of whiskey.

"Good, good." Ty had to clear the tickle from the back of his throat. "Let's try something a little harder now. Walk with her to the other side of the yard. When you get down there tell her to sit and stay. Use the hand gestures I showed you as well. And then walk back to me."

Again, Van hesitated and that hesitation caused Kaia to look to Ty for guidance. He purposely averted his gaze and waited for Van to find her confidence again.

Finally, Van did what he'd told her. She fumbled with

the hand gestures, but they were close enough that, along with the verbal commands, Kaia knew what was expected of her. And thanks to her training, she responded beautifully.

Kaia's gaze never left Van as she slowly walked back across the yard. Van stopped several feet away from Ty. The move was intentional. She'd been putting space between them since the moment he walked in the door. For the briefest moment, he thought about calling her on the bullshit.

But that wouldn't accomplish anything productive.

Clenching his jaw, Ty said, "Do you see how she's watching you? Her body is strung tight. Even from here, I can see she's vibrating with excitement and attention. That's what you want when you're working with her. And you're going to need to work with her on a regular basis. She's used to having a job. She needs that."

Van nodded stiffly.

"All right, call her to you. And don't forget to praise her when she obeys."

Van did what he said and Kaia followed her commands perfectly. But it was obvious Van felt completely out of her element. He'd hoped that as she worked with Kaia, she would get more comfortable. But almost an hour and a half into their first session she was still struggling.

Apparently, he needed to adjust his expectations.

He watched Van go through the motions for several more minutes without prompting her. When he was giving Van instructions she was okay, but on her own…she was clearly uncomfortable. And that tension was translating to Kaia, who was starting to act up.

If Van didn't get a hold of herself, Kaia was going to take over.

"Stop!" Ty finally yelled across the yard.

Kaia immediately halted, her eyes darting straight to him, her body quivering with anticipation.

Van's shoulders slumped. She blew a frustrated breath out of her mouth, fluttering the fringe of bangs hanging into her eyes. Her skin was flushed with irritation.

Not a good situation for handler or dog. "Let's take a break," Ty suggested, though it really was more of a command.

"No. I want to get this. I will get this." The determination in her voice might have been endearing if it wasn't so destructive.

"Van, sometimes it's better to know when to walk away. You can't power through everything...or be perfect at everything. Kaia's had enough for the day. She deserves a treat. Let's go for a walk."

THE TENSION WAS giving her a headache. Ty's expectations weighed on her. She was used to being top of her class, but at the moment she felt like a complete idiot.

How could she manage her ER staff with authority and ease, but not be able to command a single dog with any sense of confidence?

The more she floundered the more frustrated she became.

And the confusion she saw every time she looked into Kaia's eyes wasn't helping.

She had no idea what she was doing, and the more time she spent with Ty and Kaia, the more that was becoming obvious. While Ty commanded the dog with calm efficiency, Van was out of her element.

She didn't like that sensation at all.

Anxiety coursed through her body, an electrical current crackling across her skin.

And it didn't help that every time Ty came close, that energy doubled back on her, zapping her like she'd touched metal to a light socket.

She wanted him to touch her. She also wanted him to go away.

He did neither.

"I'll only be here a little while, Van."

She didn't need him pointing out the obvious, especially when it made her stomach feel like a hollow pit.

"I saw a park a couple blocks over when I drove in yesterday. Why don't we get a change of scenery? It'll be good for both you and Kaia."

Van nodded. What else could she do?

She'd lived in the neighborhood for almost three years now. Driven past that park thousands of times. But couldn't remember visiting once. It wasn't her kind of place, full of people and kids. Dogs. Women in their little running shorts and matching sports bras.

When she needed stress relief she preferred a nice, clean gym to exercising in the elements. Climate-controlled and structured. That's what she liked.

Whatever.

"Let me change my shoes." If they were walking, the sandals she'd slipped on weren't very practical. Sitting on the end of the bed, she pulled out her running shoes and stared at the laces as she tied double knots.

The rumble of Ty's voice reached her, not enough to understand the words, but the tone was clear. He was talking to Kaia. She could hear the animation in his voice, inflection that wasn't present whenever he talked to Van. At least not today.

Four months ago…

The memory of him looming over her in the dark, whispering words against her skin, assaulted her. Dirty words that made her blood sing. Sweet words that had her body melting. Nonsense that actually made all the sense in the world—at least, it had at the time…

Shit.

Screwing her eyes shut, Van pushed the thoughts away. They weren't productive or helpful. In fact, if she couldn't get them under control they were going to sabotage her.

A cold nose against her bare leg startled her. Her eyes popped open and looked straight into the warm brown ones staring patiently back at her.

"Good girl, Kaia," Ty said. He filled the doorway to her bedroom, his wide shoulders pressed against the jamb and his thick arms crossed over the expanse of a mus-cled chest.

Double shit.

"What are you doing in my bedroom, Ty?" The words came out much more harsh than she'd wanted, tinged with the fear that she wouldn't be able to control herself with his close proximity to her bed.

"Kaia was getting impatient. Hurry up."

His dictatorial tone made her want to snap at him, but she bit back the instinct. She would not take the bait.

Growing up, Ty had delighted in making her react. It was a game he liked to play. How quickly could he get her to lose her temper? Back then, the answer was very.

Now, she prided herself on her self-control and no one, especially Ty Colson, was going to make her lose that.

Standing up, she rested a hand on Kaia's head and spoke to the dog instead of the man. "Well, then, let's get this show on the road."

Ty turned and headed back down the hallway ahead of her. Kaia gave a little whimper, her gaze swinging back and forth between the two of them, unsure as to whom she should follow, but finally settling on a position between them.

A plastic bag swung from Ty's hand, a leash twined between his fingers. At the front door he paused long enough to reach back and clip the end onto the harness Kaia was wearing.

She tried to stay behind Ty and Kaia as they hit the sidewalk in front of her house, but Kaia kept turning around to look at her. Eventually, Ty slowed down, matching his gait to hers and placing Kaia directly between them.

The dog seemed much happier with that arrangement, so Van let it be.

They walked in silence, but that didn't stop her mind from whirling ninety to nothing.

She could feel him…the masculine vibe that emanated from his entire body. He didn't even have to try, it was just there.

He was a man. Always had been. Even as a gangly teenager, there'd been something about him…something older than any kid deserved to be.

Van racked her brain for something to talk about, but nothing seemed safe. She didn't want to discuss her brother, which meant just about every memory, friend and acquaintance they shared was off-limits. And she sure as hell wasn't going to discuss their interlude in the tree house.

Kaia's shoulder brushed against her thigh. She watched the dog's limping stride, and not for the first time felt awed by how completely she compensated for the loss of her limb.

Guilt swamped Van. She should have been paying more attention to Kaia instead of worrying about her own bad mood, and should have walked slowly so the dog wouldn't have to put in so much effort. Not that it seemed to bother her.

"She's completely healed?" Van found herself asking, although she hadn't planned on going there. Thoughts of Kaia's injuries inevitably led to thoughts of her brother's death.

"She wouldn't be here if she wasn't. She had to be medically cleared and then psychologically evaluated to ensure she could make a safe pet before the military would consider adopting her out."

"Oh."

He'd said something about that before, but Van hadn't really thought about the process. She knew it had taken some time, but just assumed most of that had been for Kaia to heal from her injuries.

"Are there any residual medical issues? Any medications? Therapy? How can I help her?"

Ty turned, his gaze spearing into hers. She got lost in those stormy-blue eyes for a second, her mind emptying of everything but him…and how he could make her body hum.

Shaking her head, Van tried to pull herself back to reality.

"Nope, she's fully healed. Nothing you need to do except love her."

Love her. Why did that thought cause nerves, grief and longing to mix uncomfortably in her belly?

They reached the park. From several feet away, someone called her name.

"Savannah! Hey, Savannah!"

She looked over to find one of her neighbors waving frantically.

Nadine lived two doors down. The week Van had moved in she'd shown up at the door with a plate of brownies and a big smile on her face. She was sweet, nosy and—it didn't take Van long to realize—the self-appointed neighborhood gossip.

"Did you hear about Mr. Macintosh? Poor thing. He shouldn't have been trying to clean those gutters himself, though. My son Eric would have been happy to help. I didn't know you had a dog. And who's this tall drink of water with you?"

Nadine finally paused, staring up at Van expectantly from where she'd crouched down to pet Kaia's head.

But before Van could answer, Ty stepped forward. "Ma'am, you should never approach a dog without permission from the owner."

"Oh." Nadine blinked and then scrambled up. "I'm sorry. I suppose you're right. I've just never met a dog I didn't like."

There was something about the mega-watt smile Nadine flashed that set Van's teeth on edge. Along with the neighborhood gossip, she was also known as the neighborhood flirt.

"What happened to the poor thing?"

Van's stomach rolled. For the first time she realized that this was a question she'd have to answer over and over again.

And that each time she did would be a reminder of Ryan. She had no idea what to say. But luckily, Ty did.

"Kaia is a retired military working dog. She was injured in the line of duty."

"Oh, the poor thing," Nadine gushed, again reaching out to touch her.

"She's been trained as an attack dog."

Van had to admit a small part of her was gleeful at the way Nadine snatched her hand back, cradling it against her chest like Kaia had snapped at her. Kaia simply sat, patiently watching the flighty woman.

With a wide-eyed glance, Nadine's gaze darted around the park full of people, taking in the mothers, fathers, grandparents and kids running, yelling and laughing.

"Is it safe to have her here?"

"Absolutely. She won't attack unless ordered to."

Nadine's wary gaze returned to Kaia. "Gosh, she looks so sweet."

"She is. One of the sweetest dogs you'll ever meet."

Nadine flashed another smile, this one a bit sickly, and then made her excuses to leave. Van watched her flit from group to group, no doubt relaying the message that Kaia was a killing machine everyone should protect their children from.

"Dammit," Van whispered under her breath.

"Not like you could keep her history a secret, Van. At least this way she'll spread the information for you so that you don't have to answer questions every time you and Kaia step out of the house."

Van looked over at Ty. He simply stared at her, understanding filling his gaze.

"Thanks."

4

TY'S LIPS QUIRKED up at the edge, his only acknowledgment of her simple words of appreciation.

It hit her hard that he understood, and without much effort, had helped her avoid an uncomfortable situation. Something soft and warm swelled inside her chest.

Not good.

Steering them over to an open field beside the park, Ty plopped down onto the thick grass. He didn't wait for her to join him before rummaging in the bag he'd brought, retrieving a floppy fabric Frisbee that had seen better days.

"What the heck is that?"

"Kaia's favorite toy."

Van settled onto the ground beside him, drawing her knees up to her chest and wrapping her arms around them. Ty unsnapped the leash from Kaia's harness. The dog's body vibrated and her gaze was glued to the Frisbee, tracking every movement.

Ty reared back and flung the toy across the field. Kaia sprang into action, her powerful body bunching as she darted after the spinning disk. Without hesitation, she bounded up and snatched it straight out of the air.

"That missing leg doesn't slow her down at all, does it?" Van said.

"Nope, not really."

She watched Ty throw the disk several times, and each time Kaia brought it back and dropped it right in front of him, panting expectantly.

Van rocked back and forth, not even aware of the motion until Ty reached out and placed a heavy hand on her knee.

"It's going to be fine."

She had no idea how that could possibly be true. Heat, his heat, seeped beneath her skin. The buzz was immediate and overwhelming. He'd only touched her leg, and for barely a few seconds, but her body felt like it had been hit with defibrillator paddles.

Uncomfortable awareness filled her. For her sanity, she needed to get away from him.

Pushing up from the ground, Van wandered closer to the playground equipment.

Kids, wrapped up in their summer fun, yelled and chased each other. On the sidelines, adults talked and watched, some read books or punched aimlessly at their phone screens.

Van let her gaze drift amongst the energy and activity. But then it stopped at the far side of the park. A guy she'd never seen before was just standing there, clearly out of place. Not that she necessarily knew all the neighbors. Or the people who normally frequented the park. But there was something about him that felt…off.

He was fidgety. His eyes kept darting around, never landing on anything for long. After watching him for several minutes, Van concluded he was alone at the park. At least, he certainly wasn't with any of the kids.

Working in the ER, she'd treated enough junkies to recognize the signs.

She felt a presence beside her. Without looking, she knew it was Ty. "Are you seeing this?" she asked.

"Yep."

She couldn't just sit there and do nothing, especially when she had the resources to help the man. Straightening her spine, Van was about to head over to him and give him her standard speech about drug treatment options, but before she'd even taken the first step Ty's hand wrapped around her arm.

"Don't."

"Don't what?"

His head swiveled and his only response was a cold, intense stare that had shivers snaking down her spine. Gone was the boy she'd grown up with, her brother's best friend, and in his place was the hardened soldier who'd spent years in the middle of a war zone. She could see the experience and knowledge swirling in his gaze.

It bothered her that anyone would ever have to deal with the things Ty had seen. But it bothered her more that the wounded boy she'd longed to protect had grown into a man scarred by even more tragedy.

But she didn't need a tortured hero; she was far from helpless. Placing her hand over his, she pried Ty's fingers from her arm. "I deal with men like that all the time, soldier. I'll be fine."

His lips thinned and his eyes narrowed to unhappy slits. He opened his mouth, probably to lambast her, but the words stalled.

A high-pitched scream split the park.

Ty swore under his breath.

Beside them, Kaia's ears pricked and her body went stiff.

"Someone stop him! That guy grabbed my purse from

the stroller." An attractive blonde woman, probably in her late twenties, was pointing at the junkie hightailing it away from the park. Several women crowded around her. Most snatched up their children and held them close. But none of them were in a position to run after the man.

Van didn't blame them. She knew from firsthand experience that addicts who were tweaking for a fix could be highly unpredictable and dangerous, and none of them had experience dealing with that kind of thing. Besides, he had a head start.

On everyone but Kaia.

She didn't see or hear the command, but it was obvious Ty had given it.

One minute Kaia was standing at his hip, the next she was streaking across the park in hot pursuit. And even with the loss of a limb, she was easily gaining on the man.

There was an audible gasp as Kaia leapt for him, snapping her jaws around his arm and holding tight as he spun on the spot, trying to dislodge her.

The man screamed, a piercing wail that sent chills down Van's spine.

With his free hand, he began pummeling Kaia around the head.

And that's when she got pissed.

Without another thought, Van took off across the park. Ty was already several steps in front of her. "Make him stop," she yelled.

Kaia wrestled the man to the ground, using the weight of her body and her sharp teeth to subdue him. Ty waded in. He must have given another command because Kaia released her hold, scooted out of the way and sat back on her haunches.

Van could see Ty had the junkie well in hand as he rolled him onto his stomach, jerked his arms up high and placed a knee on his back to immobilize him.

Van skidded to a halt beside Kaia, quickly running her hands over the dog, looking for signs of injury.

"She's fine, Van."

"He was beating the shit out of her, Ty," she spit out, anger flaring in her chest.

"She's trained for that. I promise, she's fine."

Kaia sat quietly—she wasn't even breathing hard—and let Van run her hands over every inch of her body. She stared at her with those deep brown eyes, full of calm.

A calm Van apparently needed.

She realized her own heart was racing, her stomach flipping around like someone had placed her on a roller coaster. Tears burned the backs of her eyes.

She stared into Kaia's gaze, the last piece of her brother, and realized that after only a day it would devastate her if something happened to the dog.

The thought instantly made her more antsy and unsettled.

"Someone call 911. Van, I need you over here. This guy is the one bleeding."

Van's body jolted into action. She scrambled over to kneel beside Ty. "This nice woman is an ER doctor. If you'll cooperate, I'll let you up so she can look at your wounds."

The guy moaned and nodded.

"If you try to run or do anything stupid, Kaia is right over there, just waiting to take you down again."

The guy whimpered. "Jeez man, I promise. Just keep that psycho dog away from me," he wheezed.

Van leaned down to his ear, "She isn't psycho. She's a highly trained weapon. So I suggest you move slowly and do exactly as I say."

TY WATCHED THE HULLABALOO. He'd clipped the leash back onto Kaia's harness, not because he expected her to run off or react badly to the commotion, but because, after the demonstration of her skills, the spectators had been restless.

He'd watched Van administer first aid to the junkie. And while he was a captive audience, she'd also taken the opportunity to talk to him about rehab and the options that were available for assistance in getting clean.

He really hoped the guy listened, but Ty wasn't holding his breath.

He'd spoken with the officers who'd responded to the call. In the grand scheme of things, a thwarted purse snatching wasn't a major deal. But Kaia's involvement had brought extra attention...and scrutiny.

Thankfully, with her scheduled appearance in the Fourth of July parade in a couple days, the mayor and police chief were already aware of her presence. Not to mention her skill set.

Van smacked her palm against the closed door of the ambulance and then put her hands on her hips as she watched it drive away. The guy wasn't severely injured, but he might need a stitch or two.

"You'll be in town for a few days, right?" an officer asked Ty.

He pulled his gaze away from Van and nodded. "At least through this week. Maybe next."

"I doubt we'll need to get in touch with you again. There were enough witnesses. But just in case, please make sure you provide us with your contact information before you leave."

Ty nodded and then wandered to where Van was standing with a couple of the women who'd hung around.

She looked tired. He could see lines of exhaustion creasing her forehead from several feet away.

"You ready to head back? They're done with Kaia and I'm sure she'd like some water and food."

Van nodded and gave the other women an apologetic smile. Together, she and Ty headed in the direction of her house. Kaia trotted beside, the leash slack between them.

When they reached Van's front porch, she dug in the pocket of her shorts, fishing out a set of keys. They jingled as she fumbled with them, then fell to the wooden floor with a loud clatter.

Kaia's ears pricked.

Van swore beneath her breath.

She dipped to pick them up at the same time as Ty.

Kaia scrambled backward and sideways, wrapping the leash around his back and pulling him off-balance… knocking him straight into Van.

Unstable, they both collapsed to the floor, Van stretched out haphazardly beneath him.

All the air rushed from his lungs, not from the impact, but from the feel of her beneath him once more.

His fingers let the leash slip through, tangling in Van's silky hair instead.

Her eyes flashed with need. Her lips parted, making a silent offer he was too weak to ignore.

Dipping his head, he claimed her mouth. The kiss started out soft and testing, but it didn't stay that way. The moment his lips touched hers heat ballooned up and took over. He'd meant to be gentle, but…

His tongue thrust inside the open invitation of her parted lips. His hips rolled helplessly against hers. She whimpered, her fingers tightening their grasp on his shirt.

At first he feared she might protest. But the way she responded... Her tongue tangled with his, stroking and seeking. She shifted beneath him, her thighs opening so he could settle closer.

Hell, they were going at each other on her front porch like two starved animals where God and country could walk by and see.

As much as he didn't want to, he was about to end it when Van's body language changed. Instead of grasping at him, she started pushing him away, her palms planted at his shoulders and shoving.

She tore her mouth from his, her teeth scraping against his bottom lip.

"This was a bad idea four months ago," she panted. "It's an even worse idea now. Get off me."

Ty's brain had to scramble to catch up. He felt like he was moving in slow motion as he levered himself off the ground. Reaching down, he offered a hand she refused to take.

Van brushed herself off, glaring at the floor like he'd purposely knocked her down and attacked her.

That was bullshit.

And then her words registered.

"So you do remember," he said quietly.

5

OF COURSE SHE REMEMBERED. She'd never forget that night, or the way Ty had somehow managed to give her something so good in the middle of something so bad.

But that didn't mean she was stupid enough to want him to know that. Her relationship with Ty Colson was complicated enough as it was.

But her big mouth had opened and now she didn't have much of a choice.

"I remember," she confessed.

And if she hadn't, no doubt that kiss they'd just shared would have brought memories flooding back.

Not a fan of confrontation, Van scooped up the fallen keys that had started this mess. But she didn't get anywhere close to the lock before Ty's hand squeezed around hers, pulling them out of her hand.

"Give those back," she demanded.

"Not a chance, princess." He tucked the keys into his front pocket…right next to the unmistakable bulge pressing against his zipper.

Bastard. He knew she wasn't going after them. She could turn around and walk away…to where? The park they'd just come from? No, thank you.

She didn't know her neighbors well enough to just

show up on their front steps. Her best friend Bethany, a nurse in the ER, lived on the other side of the city with her husband and two kids. She'd come if Van called, but then she'd just have to sit here with Ty and wait.

He'd get what he wanted anyway.

She growled something unpleasant beneath her breath.

His only response was a twisted smile that she immediately wanted to wipe off his face. Fortunately for him, she'd taken an oath not to harm anyone. But it was touch and go for a minute.

Turning away, Van stalked to the far side of the porch, tossing words she wanted to mean but didn't quite feel over her shoulder. "I suggest you do exactly what I plan on doing and forget that night ever happened."

She felt him way before she heard him. All that pent-up tension and heat slipping over her skin like fingers, caressing her into a reaction she didn't want to feel.

Ty didn't actually touch her, though. He didn't have to.

"You keep telling yourself that, princess," he whispered, the soft puff of his breath tickling her ear. A shiver rolled down her spine. He was too close not to notice.

He chuckled.

Van ground her teeth together, biting back words that would only cause more trouble and attempting to find a better—safer—outlet for all the pent-up energy his nearness caused.

"I remember every moment of that night," he murmured, his words low and dangerous to her equilibrium.

"Highly unlikely considering how drunk you were."

His fingertips found the curve of her neck and slowly, devastatingly, trailed across her skin. Goose bumps erupted in the wake of his touch, a telltale sign she was powerless to hide.

"I stopped drinking the minute we hit that tree house. I was sober as a judge by the time things got…heated."

"Ha!"

"The way you looked, naked, flushed with desire and spread out on that blanket, is something I'll never forget. Not as long as I live."

Her heart skipped a beat. She tried to tell herself it was because he'd indirectly mentioned dying. But she knew she was lying.

Ty swept her hair over one shoulder, exposing the curve of her neck. The warm summer breeze ghosted over her, replaced almost immediately by the blazing heat of his mouth.

She whimpered. The sound simply escaped, uncontrollable and way too revealing.

No. "I can't do this," she said, the words coming out a strangled mess. "We can't do this."

Yanking her body away from his, she tried to escape, but he'd maneuvered them both so that she couldn't.

A hand on the railing at either side of her hip, he'd left her two choices, stand and take whatever he wanted to dish out or put her hands on him and push him away.

She didn't trust herself to touch him.

Turning in the circle he'd created, Van pressed her butt tight to the railing and leaned back as far as she could. It wasn't nearly enough.

Tipping her head back, she stared up into his stormy-blue eyes. "Please, Ty, don't do this. You're only here for a few days."

His gaze raced across her face, serious and searching. She had no idea what he was looking for, but she hoped he'd be satisfied and leave her alone. She was familiar enough with the human body to recognize her own fight-

or-flight response. Her pulse was racing, her heart fluttering uncontrollably in her chest.

For the second time that day, adrenaline flooded her body. Uncertainty and need tangled together, confusing and uncomfortable.

"You responded to that kiss we just shared."

She wasn't going to lie to him. Couldn't. "Yes, but that doesn't mean it's right and you know it. I'm a doctor, Ty. I understand the amazing and complex things the human body can do. And that's what we share. Nothing more than biology, physiology."

His jaw hardened, the muscle right below the chiseled line jumping rhythmically. Despite the point she was trying to make, Van wanted to reach out and soothe it.

"You're wrong."

"It doesn't matter if I am. Ty, you're the reason my brother is dead. He never should have been in Afghanistan. He followed *you* into that life. My body might think you're God's gift to continuing the species, but my brain doesn't give a shit."

He reared back as if she'd hit him. A minute ago she'd wanted nothing more than space between them. Now that she had it…she wanted the heat of his body back.

No, her traitorous libido wanted the heat of his body back.

Part of her regretted the pain she saw lurking in his eyes…pain she'd put there. But the rest of her recognized the need to press her advantage while she had it.

"Before that night I hadn't had sex in almost a year," she continued. "And I haven't been with anyone since. It would be easy to let myself indulge in the release you're offering, but we both know that's all it would be. You'll be gone in a few days, and let's be honest, it isn't likely we'll see each other after this."

Ty's gaze hardened, his eyes like ice. In that moment she could see the ruthless, fearless, dangerous soldier that he'd become.

That man scared her. Not because she thought he might hurt her, but because it was a reminder that no matter their history, she really didn't know the man standing in front of her. Not anymore.

Fishing her keys from his pocket, Ty flipped them to her. Van scrambled to catch them.

"Take Kaia inside and be sure to give her plenty of water." His voice was flat. "I'll be back tomorrow."

Van watched him walk down her front steps to the car sitting in her driveway.

Kaia lifted up onto her haunches from where she'd been enjoying a patch of sunshine beside Van. Her ears pricked and her gaze stayed with Ty as he walked away.

She let out a single, soft sound that echoed through Van's chest.

For some goddamn reason, she felt the urge to make the same sound.

Instead, she turned away, went inside and did as Ty had said.

HE WANTED TO hit something. Something solid, something that would send pain reverberating through his body. A physical sensation he understood and could handle. Unlike the tearing sensation of grief ripping through his body.

It wasn't a new feeling. Quite the opposite in fact— he'd struggled with it from the time he was nine or ten. Being a convenient punching bag for his mother's asshole boyfriends had taught him a thing or two…not all of the lessons were good.

Luckily, he'd had Mr. Cantrell to teach him that fists were rarely the solution. Today, he wasn't sure that lesson was strong enough to stick.

Despite the punishing words Van had flung at him, his dick was still hard enough to pound nails.

If any other woman had spoken to him that way he would have turned around and never looked back. But with Van he couldn't make himself do it.

Worse, instead of making him walk away, her words had simply made him want to prove her wrong even more.

Because she was, though she didn't want to admit it.

There was a hell of a lot more between them than simple biology—there always had been. Long before things had gotten so screwed up, he'd wanted her. And not simply because she was beautiful.

Van was intelligent, confident and isolated in the same way he'd always been. It was something he'd recognized. Something they shared. Something he'd never understood since she was surrounded by people who loved her.

He was isolated because no one in his life, other than the Cantrells, had cared much about him. But Van…she was responsible for her isolation.

He'd always wondered why.

Oh, growing up, she'd had friends. Girls with whom she'd go to the mall, or have sleepovers, or whisper about boys. But she was still aloof, holding pieces of herself back.

He knew because he'd watched.

The thing was, he didn't think any of the other people in her life recognized that she was doing it. There was a part of him that wondered if Van even knew.

Back then he'd wanted to break through to her, but he'd known he wasn't the right guy for the job. Now… he still knew that, but wasn't sure it mattered anymore.

Not considering the way she'd responded to him on her front porch.

If she'd pushed him away that would have been the end of it. But she hadn't. She'd clutched at him. Opened for him. Let him in, physically at least.

She'd given him a taste and as with any good drug, he was already craving more.

So even as his head screamed at him to listen to her, he wasn't sure he had the strength.

They'd crossed a line, four months ago, and again today.

The thing was, with Van, he had to move carefully. Like a well-executed battle plan. If he wanted something from her, he'd need to be precise about how to get it.

The problem was, he wasn't entirely certain what he wanted from her.

No, that wasn't true.

He wanted her naked beneath him again, making those tiny mewling sounds that haunted his dreams. He wanted her vulnerable and passionate. He wanted her real. He wanted to wipe away the pain and regret that clouded her gorgeous green eyes.

Something told him most of those things weren't going to happen.

Ty had no idea where he was going until his car turned onto the decrepit street.

This place was a far cry from the neighborhood Van lived in, with the perfect picket fences and families.

Here paint peeled off siding. Shutters hung haphazardly, with no one caring enough to straighten them when a nail gave out. Rust covered ancient metal fencing. Weeds grew where grass should have been.

Home sweet home.

Ty pulled the car to a stop outside his mother's house. He assumed she still lived there, although he hadn't spoken to her in about twelve years. What was the point?

He should go inside.

But he wouldn't.

Again, what was the point?

They had nothing left to say to each other.

Despite everything she'd done to him—or allowed others to do to him—it'd been difficult to walk away from her. No matter how destructive the life she'd given him, she was still his mother and there would always be a part of him that wanted her to be different.

Wanted his history to be different.

But it never would be. He'd always be the little boy no one cared about. The guy who couldn't keep up in school because he was too busy working two jobs in an effort to keep food in his belly and a roof over his head.

The kid who struggled to believe he hadn't deserved all those punches to the face or kicks to the ribs, even if his adult brain promised he didn't.

Goddammit.

The last thing he needed right now was a turn down memory lane—for him, it was more like memory dark alley.

Cranking the key in his ignition, Ty decided there was somewhere else he needed to be.

This time, he knew exactly where he was headed and the reception he'd receive when he got there.

Pulling up outside the Cantrells' after visiting his own

childhood home was like breaking through a bank of fog...the world seemed clear again.

Warmth spilled from the house out across the darkened porch. Ty hesitated in the car for a second. Long enough to watch Mrs. Cantrell walk in front of the living room window, lean down and press a kiss onto Mr. Cantrell's forehead on her way to the kitchen.

Shit, *that* was what he wanted. The easy affection born from acceptance and years of shared experiences.

Something he'd never have because deep down, he knew he didn't really deserve it.

Shaking off the melancholy that was pressing in, Ty unfolded from the car and knocked on the front door.

Margaret answered, gifting him a huge smile and a warm hug, as always. Ty shifted uncomfortably in her embrace, even as he wrapped his arms around her and let her affection seep inside.

"Nick, Ty is here." She'd barely gotten the words out before she was pulling him inside. "We're already finished dinner, but I can warm you up a plate if you'd like."

"Forget dinner, go for the peach pie she's got cooling on the stove." Nick Cantrell was a big man, tall and wide. His son had taken after him, earning a scholarship to play football for a small college...until his antics had cost Ryan the free ride.

Nick's hand smacked down onto his shoulder, squeezing tight for several seconds before letting go.

"Thanks, Mrs. C, but I'm good."

"That's a mistake." Nick grinned. "She's been torturing me with the promise of that pie for the last two hours. Trust me."

Ty shook his head. "All right. A small piece."

Margaret harrumphed, which Ty knew meant he

would probably end up with at least a quarter of the pie on his plate. And he'd eat every bite.

"You boys head into the other room. I'll bring it in."

A baseball game played in the background as they settled into matching recliners. Margaret brought them each a slice of pie covered in whipped cream—not the kind from a can. She'd clearly whipped it up herself. She patted his cheek and then disappeared into the back of the house.

Ty hadn't realized just how hungry he was until the sweet scent of pastry surrounded him. Nick was right, the pie tasted like heaven. He wolfed down the entire piece in a few huge bites. Ty wasn't paying much attention to the game, and it was obvious Nick wasn't either when he reached over, punched a button on the remote and muted the sound.

"How are you, son?"

Ty turned to look at the man who'd been the only father he'd ever really known. Hearing Nick call him *son*, something he'd been doing for years, sent something warm curling through Ty's chest. Until guilt twined with it uncomfortably.

"I'm fine."

"Bullshit." Nick's lips twisted into a smile that took some of the sting out of the word.

"All right. I really don't want to be here."

"Here, here? Or in Watershed?"

"Watershed. I'm always glad to see you and Margaret." Ty's chest tightened. "Can't get peach pie like this in Afghanistan."

Nick just nodded. They were quiet for a few minutes before he said, "You wanna tell me what brought you to the door at nine o'clock at night? Not that we don't like having you here, Ty. But I know you well enough to realize something's on your mind."

Nick was right of course, but Ty didn't think he was the right person to talk with. At least, not about his mixed-up emotions where Van was concerned.

"I'm not looking forward to the parade. It's difficult enough, missing him."

Nick laughed, a tiny sound that held no humor. "You sound like Van."

Ty stiffened. The plate in his hand rattled. The reaction was involuntary and he was pissed at himself for having zero control whenever Van's name was mentioned.

"I don't suppose you two have worked anything out? Stubborn, both of you."

"What do you mean?"

Nick just looked at him with an expression Ty had been the recipient of often as a boy…usually after convincing Ryan to do something that would get them both in trouble. A look that said Nick Cantrell wasn't as stupid at Ty wanted him to be.

"That tree house is in my backyard, Ty Colson. Do you think I'm unaware of what happened between you and my daughter the last time you were home? Margaret and I were hoping you'd both finally gotten your heads out of your asses, but apparently that hasn't happened yet."

Wait. "What?"

Nick shook his head, a tiny smile tugging at the corners of his lips and creasing the outer edge of his eyes.

"You and she have been dancing around each other for years, son. Was hoping you'd finally stopped posturing and made a move."

"I got your son killed."

The thunderous reaction that crossed Nick's face now

was less familiar, and had Ty rocking back into the plush arms of the chair.

Growing up, other parents would've convinced their son that Ty was a bad influence. Mostly because he was. They would've forbidden their child to associate with him. Plenty had. But not the Cantrells. No matter what he did or how much trouble he stirred up, they always welcomed him into their home. Into their lives.

But now, Nick's expression seemed cold. It was finally coming. What he'd always known he deserved.

Except, once again Nick surprised him.

"Son, I see your head is further up your ass than I suspected. You did not get Ryan killed, and if I ever hear you say that again, you and I will have a problem. Ryan made his own choices."

The echo of Van's accusation rang through his ears, powerful and convincing, just like the insults he'd listened to over and over again as a child. "He never would have been in Afghanistan if it wasn't for me."

Nick twisted in his chair, leaned out and grasped Ty's hands, pulling him close so that he couldn't avoid the other man's gaze. "You listen to me. Ryan had his own issues to deal with. But if you think that stunt y'all pulled senior year changed his path then you don't know him. He might have gone to college and played ball for a few years, but eventually he would have ended up in the same place. He loved being a dog handler just as much as you do. He prided himself on serving his country and fighting for what we stand for. And his mother and I were proud of him. Do not take that away by implying his sacrifice wasn't a choice he made. He was his own man."

Ty swallowed. Instead of making the guilt he carried

disappear, Nick's words only increased the weight of regret. And loss.

God, he wanted Ryan back.

"It isn't the same without him," he finally whispered.

Nick's hand wrapped around the back of Ty's neck, squeezing tight. The pinch was welcome. It was a pain he could feel. Physical pain he knew how to deal with.

"I know."

"There's a part of me that doesn't want to be out there anymore, not without him. But then I think I'm a coward for thinking about leaving just because he's gone."

"There's nothing wrong with questioning if your life should take another path now. Ryan would be the first to tell you to do what feels right. Being on the front lines isn't the only way you can serve."

"Maybe not, but it's what I've trained for. Where I can do the most good."

"This isn't a decision you need to make right now. Take a few days. Enjoy your leave. And settle things between you and my daughter."

Ty laughed, the sound bursting out of him unexpectedly.

"Oh, I think things are settled. Van wants nothing to do with me."

Nick sat back into his chair, a half smile tugging at his lips. "Son, I love my daughter more than anything on this planet. But that doesn't mean I'm blind to her faults. Van doesn't know what she wants, at least not where relationships are concerned. I guess now's the time to figure out what you want...and then decide what to do about it."

6

VAN WASN'T SURE which was worse, that memories of that night four months ago made her unable to sleep for shit the last two days, or that Ty had listened to her and disappeared.

She hadn't seen him for a day and a half. She had no idea where he was or what he was doing.

And it bothered her that it mattered.

Maybe if she'd been at work she could have distracted herself, but since all she had was Kaia, her mind had begun to turn on her, playing out multiple scenarios—ones she'd encountered in the ER—for why Ty had simply disappeared. Especially after he told her he'd be back.

She'd almost convinced herself he was lying in a ditch somewhere until she spoke to her mother and found out he'd stopped by and mentioned something about running up to Lackland Air Force Base in San Antonio to see a friend at the military working dog training school.

The irritation she felt over Ty disappearing like that was ridiculous and she knew it. He'd done exactly what she'd told him to do—go away. But that did nothing to stop her from feeling…was it disappointment?

Of course, kissing her on her front porch didn't mean

he owed her anything, especially a rundown of his where-abouts.

But her lingering irritability from the encounter was only aggravated by the situation she currently found her-self in.

"Right this way, Ms. Cantrell." Julie, the cheerful, bright-eyed young woman helping to coordinate the Fourth of July parade, rushed ahead of her. She had been assigned the task of making sure Van and Kaia arrived where they were needed on time.

Julie's smile was blinding as she indicated Van should climb into the vintage convertible Mustang, which she and Kaia would be riding in for the parade.

"Jump in, girl," Van said and watched as Kaia bounded into the car. She followed, placing her feet on the back-seat and settling gingerly on the fluffy mat someone had thoughtfully laid out across the back of the open car.

At two o'clock in the afternoon it was already blazing hot. But that was no surprise for Texas in July. The sun beat down on Van's head. She'd put on an emerald-green tank that flowed around her body in the hopes that the loose, thin material would help against the heat. She'd paired it with silky black shorts and rhinestone sandals.

Cool, calm and sophisticated. Appropriate for the oc-casion and the outdoor location. But the put-together look was far from how Van actually felt.

Her skin seemed so damn tight, like she'd already got-ten sunburned. Her head throbbed incessantly, and her smile felt brittle enough to break.

She didn't want to be there, even if it was nice for the town.

Several people milled in front of the car. A banner

with information about Ryan and Kaia was propped up
a few feet away.

Van stared at the words, her stomach turning over
as she read the dates listed beneath her brother's name
and rank.

God, she couldn't do this.

Beside her, Kaia released a tiny whimper, then set her
head onto Van's lap. Her hands automatically went to the
dog's head. She'd been so wrapped up in her own misery
she'd forgotten Kaia was beside her.

The dog's wet nose pressed against Van's skin. Those
warm brown eyes rolled upward, full of concern. Van felt
the blast of it straight through her chest.

"There you are," her mother's voice floated above the
din of the crowd, releasing the pressure that had been
building unchecked inside Van's chest. "Would you look
at this crowd. Ryan would've loved this."

Van looked at her parents standing beside the car. Her
dad's arm was wrapped tight around her mother's shoulders, tucking her into the shelter of his body.

How many times had she seen her parents standing
just like that? More than she could count. The support
and protection her dad offered wasn't new in the wake
of the devastating loss of their son.

That's what she wanted, and had never found. Easy
understanding, comfort and support. It was something
that had always been there between her parents.

Her mom's eyes, the same color as her own, crinkled
up at the corners in a genuine smile. But that didn't di-
minish the pain that still lurked there.

This was a difficult moment for her parents as well.
And somehow that helped. Not that she wanted their

pain, but that if they had to experience it, at least they could share it.

"Here we are," Van said, rubbing her fingers through Kaia's fur.

"Now that you've got her settled, you should bring her by the house," her dad said, nodding his head toward the dog.

"I will."

"Mr. Colson, you'll sit here beside Ms. Cantrell," Julie said, her smile still beaming wide as she approached the car from the other side. Her eyes were glued on Ty, holding the convertible's door open for him to climb in and sit beside Van.

Ty took a seat, his large body taking up more than half of the small ledge they were supposed to share.

Kaia, wedged between them, shifted, settling her head onto Ty's massive thighs.

Traitor.

Ty ran his hands down Kaia's back, digging his fingers in and kneading in a way the dog obviously loved as she stretched into the stroke.

Van's body gave an involuntary shiver. She remembered those fingers digging into her skin, massaging, caressing and stroking.

"Nick, Margaret, it's good to see you."

Her parents smiled up at Ty. "You too, son."

"We'll be starting in five minutes," a loud voice boomed out over the chaos of people, floats, music and chatter filling the space around them.

"We best go and find a spot to watch."

"You're sure you wouldn't rather ride with us?" Van asked, hating herself for the edge of desperation she couldn't seem to stop from slipping into her voice.

Having her parents there as a buffer might keep her from doing or saying something she'd regret.

"Oh, no. There isn't enough room. Besides, I'd much rather watch. We'll wave when we see you!" her mom said, grabbing her dad's hand and tugging him back into the crowd surging around them.

Alone, Ty shifted. His hand left Kaia's back and flattened onto the rear of the car, his thumb briefly brushing the curve of her ass. Van jolted, her body stiffening. Beside her, Kaia reacted as well.

"Easy."

She wasn't sure whom Ty was addressing, but his soft, soothing voice had the opposite effect than he'd probably intended.

Energy and awareness tingled beneath her skin, heat shooting out from where he'd accidentally—it was an accident, right?—touched her, flooding the rest of her body.

Searching for a distraction, Van asked, "How was your trip to Lackland? Mom mentioned you went."

"It was good. Always nice to reconnect with friends. I haven't seen Finn McAllister in years. We served together when Ryan and I first got into the program. Finn came back to work in the training unit at Lackland, but has recently been working with the drug task force in San Antonio. Interesting work."

She wanted to respond, but the words wouldn't come.

Then the car lurched forward, not fast, but enough to jolt her body. Ty's hand clamped around her hip, holding her in place.

Van's startled gaze flew to his. His blue-gray eyes were enigmatic as he watched her. There was something about them that had always captivated her.

Nope. Not today.

Scooting out of his hold, Van pulled her attention back to the front. She pasted a smile on her face and waved as they rounded the first corner and were greeted by the cheering crowd of people lining the curb.

It felt like the entire town had gathered. People stood five or six deep, crushed against each other. Little kids were perched atop their fathers' shoulders, trying to get a clear look at the passing floats.

Kaia shifted beside her, a little restless as she attempted to find a comfortable position.

Van set her hand on Kaia's shoulder. She could feel the tension trembling through her body.

"Is she okay?" Van asked, without actually looking at Ty.

He shifted, putting a protective arm around Kaia and running a soothing hand down her back. "Easy, girl," he murmured. "She's trained to handle crowds and loud noises, so she should be fine."

His words were reassuring, but the crease between his eyebrows wasn't.

They continued along the route, waving and smiling, turning and shifting but not touching. Ty kept a hand on Kaia and after a little while, the tension seemed to ease from the dog's body.

Under the blazing sun, it didn't take long for sweat to start collecting at the nape of Van's neck and beneath her breasts. The light breeze that stirred as the car moved was welcoming, but not nearly enough to combat the sun beating down on them.

Kaia's tongue started lolling out as she panted.

"I should have brought water."

Ty reached into the backpack he'd stowed on the backseat and pulled out a collapsible bowl and a bottle of water. Flipping her a small smile, he poured some in, then set it on his thigh for Kaia.

The dog lapped it up like she'd been stuck in the desert for weeks without water.

"Great. Now I feel like even more of an ass."

"No, you're just not used to having a dog. You'll get the hang of it soon enough."

Suddenly, the car came to a stop. Van glanced around and realized they were in the middle of 2nd Ave, the main road leading through downtown. Bleachers had been set up in a parking lot and a raised dais rested right in front of them.

A guy with a mic and a bunch of technical-looking equipment sat in the middle of it.

Suddenly, his voice boomed out over the crowd.

"Ladies and gentlemen, the city of Watershed is proud to present Ty Colson, an active duty K-9 handler with the US Army, Savannah Cantrell, sister to Ryan Cantrell, the posthumous grand marshal for today's parade, and Kaia, the Belgian Malinois who served with Staff Sergeant Cantrell. Kaia stayed by his side during the IED explosion that claimed Mr. Cantrell's life, refusing to leave despite her own injuries."

A lump formed in Savannah's throat. Her eyes burned as her gaze swept across the crowd in front of them. They stared back, a sea of sad and pitying expressions. Dammit, this was exactly what she'd wanted to avoid.

The announcer said something Van didn't catch and a cheer shot through the crowd. Someone started chanting Kaia's name. Van supposed that was better than Ryan's.

Beside her, Kaia whimpered and shifted, tension filling her body once more.

Ty's hand pressed down on her head, rubbing behind her ears.

Standing, Van joined Ty in waving at the crowd. What else could she do?

"Ma'am, sir, if you'll sit back down we'll keep going," their driver said.

Plopping back down, she murmured, "When will this be over?"

"It won't be long." This time, Ty's soothing hand landed on her thigh. He stroked, electricity chasing after the touch. Her entire body clenched. Physically, she wanted more, even if her brain wanted him to leave her alone.

Ty simply watched her, his own gaze ripe with turmoil as they stared at each other.

One minute she'd been mired down with inaction, and the next it felt like the world erupted around her.

Somewhere in the crowd a series of loud explosions went off, *pop, pop, pop.*

Firecrackers.

Beside her, Kaia bolted to her feet. Before either of them could react, her long body was sailing over the side of the car. She stumbled as her paws landed onto the pavement.

Ty lurched after her, his body sprawled across Van's lap, half in and half out of the still moving vehicle. Instinct had her wrapping her fingers into the waistband of his uniform slacks.

The car screeched to a halt.

Several people in the crowd screamed.

Ty pushed off of Van's lap and vaulted out of the car after Kaia, a string of curse words trailing in his wake.

Van felt the same way.

She scrambled out behind him.

Ty was fast, but Kaia was faster and she seemed to be on a mission. The crowd parted, or tried to, as she wove through a maze of legs.

Parents snatched their children out of the way, panic and fear stamped across their faces as if they expected the dog to attack at any moment.

Yes, she was big and probably wild-eyed. But didn't they realize Kaia was scared?

Apparently not.

And it didn't help when her solid body collided with a toddler, probably no more than three or four, knocking the little girl backward onto the pavement. There was a muted thud and a gasp from the people around them.

Kaia didn't even slow down. Her body bounced off the child, but she just kept going, running as if her life depended on it.

Ty was in a flat-out sprint ahead of Van. If she had the time to stop and think about it, she would have marveled at the speed that large, muscled body could move at.

But that wasn't what she cared about right now. All that mattered was Kaia.

Behind her the announcer, his voice high-pitched despite the calming words he was spouting, attempted to get control of the crowd.

Knowing that she didn't really have a chance to catch Kaia, but hoping Ty did, Van dropped to her knees beside the little girl.

"Are you okay?"

Tears streamed down her upturned face. Her green eyes were huge as she stared up at Van and shook her head.

"What hurts?" she asked even as her hands started running over the child, looking for any indication of injury.

"My bum," the little girl said in an adorable voice. "That big dog knocked me down."

Van was fairly certain the girl was fine, just scared from the surprise of being bowled over by a seventy-five-pound dog. Not that she blamed her.

The girl's mother put her hand on Van's shoulder. "I think she's fine. Just startled."

An understanding smile stretched across the other woman's face.

"I'm a doctor. Savannah Cantrell in the book. If she seems dizzy or starts complaining that her head hurts or her vision is blurry, please call me and I'll meet you at the emergency room."

The woman nodded.

Van offered the little girl a quick smile, swept it over to include her mother and then stood up.

Ty was gone, which meant Kaia was long gone.

But someone pointed her in the right direction and Van took off.

SHIT, HE SHOULD have known better. Should have anticipated Kaia's nerves and especially her reaction to those damn firecrackers. It was a good thing he was preoccupied with finding her or he might have stopped to knock some sense into adolescent heads.

Not that they understood what they'd done.

Dammit.

Kaia was on a tear, and even missing a leg she was faster on her feet than he was. It didn't help that she'd had a head start and the chaos of the crowd had slowed him down. But he'd still managed to track her for several blocks.

Until he'd lost her near the outskirts of downtown.

She wasn't familiar with the area. Ty stopped, glancing around, hoping to find some clue as to which direction she might've gone.

The logical answer was home. She'd been at Van's house long enough to understand it held safety and shelter. He pulled out his cell, ready to call Van and tell her to head home to wait when a car squealed around the corner and pulled up beside him.

Van leaned out the open window. "Get in."

Ty didn't argue. He ran around the hood of the car and hopped into the passenger seat.

"I lost her."

"I'm sorry I didn't keep up, but I stopped to check on the little girl Kaia knocked over. She'll be fine."

"I'm glad she's okay."

"Any idea where Kaia might be?"

Ty shook his head. "She's not familiar with the area. I'm hoping she can scent her way back home."

"That's a long way, Ty."

"Not for Kaia. She's used to long marches in the heat, just like any good soldier."

Van looked over at him. Her fingers gripping the wheel had turned white with tension. Concern filled her deep green eyes and he felt the need to say, "I'm sorry."

"For what?"

"Not anticipating the problem."

"Ty, you're pretty badass, but not even you can predict the future."

"I should have. Her body might be fully healed, but apparently she's still struggling with some aftereffects of the explosion."

"PTSD?"

Ty nodded. It was probably the correct diagnosis,

but he didn't like the term. No soldier really did. They were big and tough. Could handle anything. Until they couldn't. And no one, he didn't care who you were, liked to admit that they weren't in control of their own emotions or reactions.

"Call Mom and Dad and ask them to go back to my place in case she shows there. We'll take the long way home and see if we can't find her along the way."

It was the best plan. Ty rolled up onto his hip so he could pull his cell out of his pocket, but stopped halfway up when Van's hand landed on his thigh.

She didn't take her eyes off the road, despite the fact that she was doing about fifteen down the residential street. The heat from her hand seeped into his skin, spreading like wildfire and igniting him from the inside out.

Ty fought the urge to bring his own hand down over hers, holding her in place.

"We'll find her. Everything will be fine."

Her words washed over him. Had anyone ever said that to him before? He couldn't remember.

He needed to change the subject before he said or did something they'd both regret.

"Badass, huh?"

Van just rolled her eyes, but a grin played at the corners of her lips.

7

THEY'D BEEN DRIVING around town for almost an hour. Her parents had called to tell them they were at Van's, but there was no sign of Kaia. With that covered, they agreed that staying out to look was the best course of action.

There was no way Van could've sat at home waiting... and Ty definitely wouldn't have handled that well.

As it was, Ty was a big bag of nerves. He hid it well, but she noticed the signs of his agitation. The way his fingers kept strumming across his thighs. The hard line of his jaw. The hyperalert way his gaze scanned around, looking for any sign or clue.

A sound blasted through the car, startling Van. She'd turned off the radio and rolled down the windows so they could listen, although she wasn't entirely certain what she'd hoped to hear. Maybe the jangle of Kaia's tags.

Instead, Ty's cell phone had broken the silence.

"Margaret, is she there?"

Van could hear the anxiety in Ty's voice. It had gotten tighter and tighter the more time had passed.

He listened. Van slowed the car in case she needed to turn around and head for home. Ty glanced over at her and gave a single, hard jerk of his head, *no*. His mouth thinned into a flat line and his eyes went dark and stormy.

Her stomach churned. She'd been the bearer of enough bad news to recognize the signs. This wasn't going to be good.

"Yes, ma'am, we'll head over there right now."

Ty punched angrily at his phone, disconnecting the call. His arm dropped into his lap and his head fell back against the headrest. His eyes screwed shut for a second before he reached up and pressed both palms into his sockets, rubbing hard.

"Well?" she asked, anxious to hear what was up.

"Head to the cemetery."

"What?"

"Apparently, the entire town has organized a search party for Kaia and someone called your mom to say she'd been spotted at the cemetery."

Oh, shit.

"Why would she go there?"

Yes, in the grand scheme of things, the cemetery wasn't that far from the parade route. They hadn't driven close because the layout of the streets had naturally funneled them in the opposite direction. But Kaia wasn't in a car, she was on foot and it was a straight shot through an industrial area, across the city park and straight into the back of the cemetery.

"She has an excellent sense of smell; it's one of the reasons her breed is good for military work."

Van closed her eyes. "My parents and I went by his grave this morning. I left Kaia in the car, but Mom took several of Ryan's things and left them on his headstone. They were in the car with us. I was so wrapped up in my own misery, I didn't even think about how that might have affected Kaia."

Ty's hand brushed across her shoulder, beneath her

hair, and cupped the nape of her neck. Tingles shot down her spine, but they were secondary to the other emotions swirling inside her.

She'd been careless.

"You live and learn, Van. Stop beating yourself up for being human."

That was easy for him to say. Ty had always laughed in the face of expectation. Growing up, she didn't think there was a rule he hadn't broken, if only to say he'd done it. And because it was easier to let everyone think nothing could touch him.

But Van had lived in fear of getting in trouble. Of the consequences that came with being less than perfect.

Even now, her worst nightmare was the thought of screwing up at work and hurting someone…or killing them. It was something she tried to push away, but never quite disappeared. It just lurked. And probably always would.

Why couldn't she be more like him? Confident and sure. Able to let things—especially unimportant ones—slip off his back?

It didn't take long to reach the cemetery. She'd been here way too often over the past few months. At first, she'd avoided the headstone that marked Ryan's last resting place. But a couple months after the service, after a really rough day at work, she'd been mindlessly tired and somehow found her car parked along the road that wound through the property.

That first time she'd just sat in the car, letting her entire day play through her head. The second time she'd gotten out of the car and leaned against the hood. The third time she'd walked straight up to his grave, crossed her arms and cursed at him for getting himself killed.

After that, whenever she had a difficult day, she'd find herself there, just talking to him.

She missed the big brother who'd always seemed to have all the answers.

But right now she couldn't think about that. She had to concentrate on caring for the dog who'd mattered so much to Ryan.

Kaia needed her.

That more than anything kept her moving forward.

Turning a corner on the paved road, Van could see her. Kaia's big body was stretched out, lying across the grass that had grown over Ryan's grave.

Her head was resting on her one front leg, her nose facing the stone. Waiting.

Van's heart broke. It was a familiar sensation, but somehow far more acute today.

The slam of Ty's car door as he got out made Van jump. The sound felt loud, inappropriate considering what had sent Kaia running.

Kaia's body twitched. Slowly, her head moved, just enough so that those big brown eyes could take them in as they approached.

Ty, ahead of Van by several steps, began talking in a low, soothing voice. Words of comfort and reassurance. How many times had she used a similar tone with a scared patient in the ER?

He closed in, crouching down beside Kaia. Slowly, he moved his hands over her body, methodically checking for any sign that she was injured…at least injured physically.

After the way Kaia had reacted to those firecrackers, it was obvious she was carrying plenty of emotional scars. Just like the rest of them.

When he was satisfied she wasn't hurt, Ty plopped down onto the grass beside her. He stretched out, pillowing his own hands behind his head.

The sight of the dog and the man together, with that stark gray stone standing tall behind them, sent something sharp lancing through Van's chest.

"What's your plan? To stay out here with her all night?" Her voice was harsh, and yet weak. Filled with emotion she didn't want to feel, but couldn't stop.

It hurt. The whole thing hurt.

And she was so damn tired of hurting.

"Nope. That would just be asking for trouble. Fourth of July and all. Considering her reaction to a firecracker, she's likely to lose her mind when the rest of the fireworks start going off later tonight."

Shit. She hadn't even thought that far ahead.

"Okay, so what *is* the plan?"

"I'm going to sit here with her for a few minutes until I'm sure she's calm and then we're going to take her home. We'll deal with tonight when it comes."

We'll. Not her and Kaia. Not even him and Kaia. The three of them together.

There was a part of her that instinctively wanted to protest, to tell him she didn't need his help. To push him away and give herself the space she desperately needed. But the fruitless act of bravado would only hurt Kaia.

And Van wasn't willing to do that.

The dog had been through enough today. So Van would ignore her own aches and pains if it meant doing what Kaia needed. She bit her tongue and nodded her head.

Crossing her arms over her chest, Van stared down at the man and the dog. She tried not to let her gaze stray to the headstone sitting silently, just a few feet away. But it was difficult.

Ryan Nicholas Cantrell
Beloved son, brother and soldier.

The words were simple. Maybe too simple. They did a poor job of summing up her brother's life. His sense of adventure and unwavering loyalty. The way he'd take up any cause when he felt like someone was being taken advantage of…a trait he'd picked up from Ty, actually.

It did nothing to convey the sound of his laughter or the way he'd tormented her the first time she'd gone out on a date. Nor did it touch on the way he'd consoled her when that same boy had broken her heart four months later, making her laugh even through her tears by offering to break the guy's kneecaps.

And, yet, they were the most important words about his life. He had been loved, by everyone who knew him.

Reaching behind him, Ty pulled the baseball cap that her mother had left just this morning off the edge of the memorial.

"God, I remember this hat. He wouldn't take the damn thing off during senior year."

A choked laugh slipped through Van's tight throat.

She watched Ty's hands, hulking and strong, bend and straighten the bill. It was from Baylor University… where Ryan had planned to play until their stupid stunt cost him his football scholarship.

Ryan was good, but not good enough to overcome the bad publicity of an arrest, even if the charges had eventually been dropped. Mostly because everyone knew they'd been guilty.

"I really wish I could go back and do it all over again. I never would have told him what I was planning that night."

No, she couldn't do this. Not right now. Not here.

Turning on her heel, Van headed for the car, but Ty's words followed her anyway.

"You know, I didn't even ask him to come with me. I was just telling him what I was going to do. And he... showed up. I tried to argue with him. I mean, it was my problem to deal with. My crusade. But it didn't matter."

No, it wouldn't have.

Her feet refused to move. They just stopped, and despite the fact that she wanted to run away—as Kaia had done earlier—she couldn't make her body respond.

Instead, she found herself turning back to the man, the dog and the headstone she couldn't escape. She wanted to scream at Ty. If he'd just kept his big mouth shut, they wouldn't be here right now, at her brother's grave. Van's gaze pulled to Kaia. With her brother's wounded dog.

"Like he would have let you do that alone."

The idiots.

During a class project sophomore year, Ty had become involved with a local animal shelter. They were severely understaffed, underfunded and overrun with animals. Whenever he wasn't working or at school, chances were you could find him at the shelter.

Van had thought the shelter provided him an escape; the dogs and cats he took care of gave him unconditional love and affection when he rarely received that from anyone else in his life.

It didn't matter that he did the grunt work, cleaning cages, washing dogs, scooping litter. Ty did it without complaint and without compensation.

The staff at the shelter were great…until the manager left and the city brought on someone new. The guy had taken one look at the overcrowding and decided a large number of the animals needed to be euthanized.

Ty had a fit, campaigning tirelessly to stop the intended killing. He even organized half the school to show up at a city council meeting, begging them to pass a law making the shelter no-kill. He managed to delay the action for a little while, but it was inevitable. The city just didn't have the funds to provide for the animals.

Van had watched frustration and anger build inside Ty, recognizing both emotions as a facade covering up the grief and pain he was so adept at hiding. And she was frustrated because there was nothing she could do to help him.

The night before the vet was scheduled to come and put the animals down, Ty broke into the shelter and took them, in a last-ditch effort to save their lives.

Loading twelve dogs into the back of his pickup, he and Ryan drove them to the outskirts of town and set them free.

No, it wasn't the best option, but in their minds it was better than watching them die.

But an eyewitness came forward, so they were quickly caught. And so were the animals, eventually being put down anyway.

That was the heartbreaking part. Watching Ty and Ryan both pay for the attempt when it was fruitless.

The staff at the shelter, everyone but the manager, had all showed up in court to lobby for Ty and Ryan.

The judge had decided to be lenient, charging them with a misdemeanor and sentencing them to community service.

No one could have anticipated the ripple of repercussions for Ryan's life.

There was the rub. Van wanted to be so pissed with both Ty and Ryan. Had even managed it for several years. But how could she stay angry with either of them when their hearts had been in the right place? They'd done something seriously stupid, but they'd done it for the right reasons.

If she was being honest, she'd actually stopped blaming Ty years ago, recognizing that Ryan had been old enough to make his own choices, regardless of the consequences. But she'd used the incident to keep Ty at arm's length. To protect herself from the certain heartache that would come from giving in to her conflicting emotions.

Ty sighed, murmured, "I'm sorry," and then replaced the hat on the headstone. It was clear those words weren't meant for her, but they still reverberated through her body like a punch.

Pushing to his feet, Ty looked down at Kaia and issued the command to heel.

She just rolled those deep brown eyes up at him and stubbornly stayed put.

A frown tugged at his full lips. "Kaia, heel," he said again, his voice with a harder edge.

This time, the dog dropped her gaze to the ground, as if she could ignore him if she didn't see him.

Hooking a hand into Kaia's harness, Ty gently pulled. Kaia resisted, using the weight of her body to stay right where she was. Ty pulled harder, raising her up onto her haunches.

Kaia's body went limp and she whimpered.

The knot Van had been fighting since they drove up

grew to the point where she felt like it was choking her. She couldn't breathe.

Bending down, Ty scooped Kaia into his arms.

She didn't struggle. She just lay lifelessly against his body. As Ty turned, her head tracked, her gaze lingering on Ryan's grave.

"Open the door for me," Ty said, his voice low and gruff.

Van rushed ahead, opened the door to the backseat and turned in time to watch the man stride across the soft green grass, a seventy-five-pound dog cradled in his arms like she weighed no more than a teacup Chihuahua.

But the expression on his face nearly killed her. Every bit of pain he was feeling splashed across his features. Grief cut grooves around his mouth. And his stormy-blue eyes raged with turmoil.

It wasn't the first time Van had seen that expression on his face. Hell, the boy she'd known had been no stranger to pain—both physical and emotional.

But it looked out of place on a man who now carried such strength and confidence.

Maybe it was the innate healer inside her, but she wanted to make it better.

He set Kaia gently onto the seat, made sure she was comfortable and then closed the car door.

Standing, he pressed his hands against the roof of the car and hung his head. Weariness coated him like a blanket.

Reaching for him, Van cupped his cheek in her palm and turned his face so she could look straight into his eyes. The agony there nearly had her knees buckling.

Four months ago he'd been there for her, giving her

exactly what she'd needed at the moment she'd been her weakest. Could she do any less for him right now?

Pushing up onto her toes, Van pressed her mouth to his.

The kiss was sweet, soothing. The gift of simple comfort. At least, it started out that way.

But one moment she was offering him solace, and the next her back was pressed against the side of the car and his hard body was flush against hers.

Her head spun. They touched from shoulders to hips to knees.

He was demanding. Heat. Need. He poured everything inside her, all the pent-up frustration, grief and passion.

She could feel herself losing control. *As if she'd ever really had it to begin with.*

Her body went liquid, giving him a soft place to land. Her fists curled into his shirt. And she opened for him.

Whatever he needed, she'd give.

They were both panting when he finally pulled back. His forehead pressed to hers, he whispered against her lips, "We need to get Kaia home."

8

THE ENTIRE WORLD was out of control. *Hell*.

Nick's words from the other day echoed through Ty's head as he sat in Van's passenger seat heading for her house.

What did he want?

His body wanted Van. Clearly, since his dick was throbbing incessantly from nothing more than a few powerful kisses.

But his brain knew he should keep his hands off her. The Cantrells were the only family he really had. By some miracle, they didn't seem to blame him for Ryan's death, even though everyone knew he was indirectly responsible. If he messed with Van...

And, when it got right down to it, there was no longevity in whatever this was between them.

Van was intelligent, forthright, so much better than he was. And her friendship, even if he'd screwed it up years ago, was important to him.

She was Ryan's little sister. So he needed to keep his goddamned hands to himself and concentrate on his reason for being here in the first place—Kaia.

Twisting, Ty took in the dog stretched across the backseat. She was miserable. You didn't need to be an expert dog handler to know that. Her eyes were sad and down-cast, her body language lethargic and listless.

Pulling into the garage, Van shot from the car. It was difficult to miss the rosy flush of passion that still colored her creamy skin. She avoided looking straight at him. Ty wanted to crowd her up against the wall, right then and there beside the spotless workbench with the tools neatly organized above.

Instead, he went to the backseat and reached in for Kaia.

She didn't protest or attempt to jump out of his arms, something that told him just how upset she really was. Her tags jangled as her head settled against his shoulder. She was big and heavy, but Ty barely noticed as he followed Van inside.

The large crate he'd brought in a couple days ago had been set up in the living room. The door stood open, the bottom covered in soft blankets with a camo pattern.

Ty set Kaia down, glanced at the bedding and then at Van. Raising a single eyebrow, his lips quirked up into a half smile.

"What? I thought maybe it would be familiar. Make her feel more at home."

"Savannah Cantrell, underneath that take-no-nonsense, straight-laced exterior you're just a huge softy."

She made a rude sound in the back of her throat, turned and disappeared into the kitchen. A minute later she reappeared with Kaia's bowls, one filled not with dog food, but shredded chicken, peas and carrots.

"You're going to spoil her," he warned.

"You say that like it's a bad thing." Her tone taunted him to say more.

Instead, Ty ducked his head to hide the smile he couldn't avoid.

Kaia sniffed at the bowl when Van set it beside her, but didn't eat. Instead, she walked into the kennel and curled up, her head on her front leg.

It was almost dark, the last rays of bright sunshine bleeding through the curtains to splash across the hardwood floor.

"Anything I need to watch for tonight?" Van asked, her arms crossed protectively over her chest.

She was putting up walls. He should let her. It was the best thing for both of them. But for some reason, the signs that she was pulling away made him want to smash through them even more.

"Not really, since I'm not leaving."

"What do you mean you're not leaving?"

"Do you really think, after what happened today, that I'd leave either of you alone? Van, she freaked out at a single firecracker. I can't imagine Watershed has changed all that much in the years I've been gone. In a few hours the entire place is gonna be lit up like a ninety-year-old's birthday cake."

Van's mouth tightened. Her shoulders stiffened. He could see the protest forming on her lips, was already waiting to counter it, but it never came.

"Fine. But I'm not entertaining you."

"If that's your way of saying you're not sleeping with me, I'm already aware of that. If that's your way of saying you're not interested in killing time by surfing through old movies on Netflix, that's also fine. I'm a big boy, Van. I can take care of myself."

Something flashed through her eyes, a bright flare that was there and gone before he could really analyze it.

"Good."

"Great."

"But I suppose we both have to eat."

He watched as she bit her lip thoughtfully. "Eventually," he said.

"You stay with her. I'll see what I can come up with for dinner."

She didn't wait for his response before disappearing again into the kitchen. He really wanted a drink, but something told him it would be smarter to wait a little while before following her.

Dropping down to the floor beside Kaia, Ty reached inside the cage and slowly stroked down her soft fur.

"I don't suppose you have any wisdom to share, you know, being a woman and all."

Kaia just rolled her soft brown eyes up to him. She snuffed, her entire body rising and falling with the motion.

"Yeah, my thoughts exactly."

THE NIGHT HAD been interminable. Van had thrown together a warm grilled chicken salad for dinner, wasting more time than necessary in the kitchen.

She'd needed the space—not to mention the relief from Ty's physical presence in her home.

After that kiss they'd shared at the cemetery...her body's signals were definitely going haywire.

Part of her wanted to ask Ty what happened now. The rest of her wasn't ready for the answer.

So she'd curled into one of the side chairs in her den, flipping on the TV to watch some mindless show followed by some special highlighting the Fourth of July program in Boston. It didn't matter which channel she picked, they were all showing the same thing. In deference to Kaia, Van muted the sound.

Which only made the tension seeping into the room worse.

Her entire body felt strung tight, ready to burst at the softest touch.

Assuming that touch came from Ty's hands.

What bothered her more than anything was that he seemed completely oblivious.

He was perfectly content to sit on her sofa and shovel the food she made into his mouth—only pausing long enough to praise her culinary skills and thank her for feeding him. He didn't make any attempts to fill the silence with chit-chat or mindless drivel.

Normally, that would have been a good thing. Her life was so hectic that when she did have a few minutes of downtime, she liked to just…breathe.

That was one reason her relationship with Justin had never really worked. He was constantly talking, telling her trivial details about his day and life that, in the face of whatever life-and-death situation she'd dealt with that day, just didn't seem to matter. And then he'd get pissed when she told him she'd rather just be alone.

Ty didn't seem to care.

The problem was, the more time they spent together, the more she became aware of him as a man, not just the boy she remembered.

The quiet way he coaxed Kaia out of her cage, tempting her to take bites of his own dinner since she hadn't touched hers. The confident, comforting way he handled her, constantly looking for signs of distress.

Kaia had finally started to come back out of the funk she'd fallen into after the parade, when an explosion out on the street had them all jumping. Well, her and Kaia. Ty didn't react at all.

Van didn't want to contemplate what that said about the environment he was used to.

"You're all right, girl."

Kaia shifted, clearly uncomfortable. The screaming whine of fireworks followed by a loud explosion and a burst of color that flashed across the front windows sent the dog skittering off the sofa.

Upset, she was unbalanced when she jumped. Her good leg collapsed beneath her. Her upper body slammed into the floor. She let out a pained yelp that had Van bolting from her chair.

But Ty beat her there.

Reaching down, he tried to grab her harness and pull her up, but Kaia turned on him.

She scrambled backward, lodging herself into the corner of the room. Unfortunately, it was right next to the front wall. Streaks of red, blue, gold and green kept flashing over her trembling body. With each loud pop from the street, she flinched and quivered.

On silent feet, Ty scooted closer. He tried again, reaching out a hand for her.

Kaia snapped her jaws—a warning. She was careful not to actually connect with Ty's hand. But the ensuing growl sent a chill down Van's spine.

Kaia's eyes, just moments ago so calm, were now fierce and hard with determination.

"Easy, girl," Ty said, holding out his hands. "I know it's scary. Trust me. I know it sounds just like that small, dark village that night. The fireworks make my heart race, too. But we're both safe."

His words rushed over Van, making her muscles

tighten and her heart clench. He hadn't shown a single sign of reaction. He was so damn good at hiding it.

She hated that he'd had to learn those skills. That he couldn't just be open about his fears.

In that moment she decided if she had anything to say about it—and she did—Kaia would never feel unsafe again.

Ty, on the other hand…there was nothing she could do to change his past. Or keep him safe now. Whenever he left, it would be to return to one of the most dangerous places in the world. And that scared the shit out of her.

In that moment, she wanted to wrap her hands in his shirt, shake him until he actually listened to her and then beg him never to go back into the line of fire.

Instead, she bit down on her tongue, stopping the rush of words that threatened to spill out. And just watched.

Slowly, Ty reached for Kaia again. He started by setting his hand on her head. Gently, deliberately, he eased his palm back, barely ruffling her fur as he went.

He didn't stop to grab her harness the first time. Instead, he went over and over the same path, whispering soothing words, just as she'd seen him do earlier in the day.

But unlike earlier, it didn't help. Kaia tensed with every burst of color splashed across the windows.

"We need to get her away from the windows and shield her from the sound as much as possible," Ty said in the same, soothing tone he'd been using.

"The bathroom in the master suite. It's at the back of the house, as far away from the street as you can get, and there aren't any windows."

"Perfect."

Ignoring the warning growl, Ty scooped Kaia into his

arms and strode across the living room. He didn't even slow down when he crossed the threshold to her bedroom, but headed straight for the attached master bath.

The room was one of the main reasons she'd purchased the house. It was huge with one of those tiled showers you could walk straight into with programmable jets that streamed out from the walls. In the far corner was a deep tub. The toilet and double trough sinks were on the opposite wall. And her favorite part, the connected walk-in closet.

"Nice," Ty grunted. Part of her was affronted at his subdued appreciation of her space. The rest of her realized he was a man, one probably more accustomed to sand and heat than iridescent tile and modern fixtures.

Dropping to the floor, Ty settled onto the rug with his back against the tub.

Van watched as his long legs stretched out into her space. This room had always seemed huge to her, which she liked. With Ty there it suddenly felt way too small.

He didn't unwrap his arms from around Kaia, but set her big body on the floor next to him, cradling her head in his lap.

Switching from one foot to the other, Van had no idea what to do. Stay or leave them alone?

She hated being unsure. Was not used to the experience, and, frankly, didn't particularly like it.

Ty saved her from the confusion. "Come sit next to us."

Unsure it was the wisest move, she did it anyway. Sinking down on the opposite side of Kaia, Van let her legs brush against the dog's soft body.

Kaia shifted, moving her paw so that it rested on Van's lap.

Glancing over at Ty, Van caught the flash of his smile before his gaze dropped to the dog between them.

Kaia was constantly bridging the gap. The single line that connected them and drew them together when the smart thing would have been to just go in opposite directions.

Van's stomach twisted at the realization. She shifted, ready to do just that and put some space between them.

But Ty's words stopped her. "I'm going to move Kaia's crate in here. It's familiar and comforting. She was looking for shelter, which is why she backed into the corner earlier."

"Shelter from what? Is it just the fireworks or is there more?"

Van realized it was the wrong question to ask at the expression of despair and grief that flashed across Ty's face. It wasn't there long before a blank mask settled back over the sharp, handsome features of his face.

In some ways, she preferred the grief to the emptiness. At least the grief was honest.

"That night, Ryan, Kaia, Echo and I had been clearing a section of road through a small village in the Helmand province. It was taking us a while. Between us and the specialized equipment the EOD unit uses, we'd already cleared a handful of IEDs. It was late. We were all getting tired. But the goal was to finish the stretch of road so the convoy could reach a camp on the other side."

Part of her wanted to stop him. She didn't need the details about her brother's death.

And yet, she did. Several times over the last few months she'd woken in a cold sweat from nightmares about Ryan's death. Without really knowing, her brain had imagined plenty of horror, often merging the worst trauma she'd seen in the ER with the few details she had of the actual event.

Maybe hearing the truth would help.

"There were hundreds of soldiers depending on us to do our jobs so that they could do theirs.

"Earlier in the day, the convoy had taken fire from a group of insurgents hiding in the mountains close by, but once we'd reached the village the volley of bullets had stopped.

"Maybe we'd grown complacent. One minute everyone was trudging along, doing their job, and the next all hell broke loose."

Ty shifted, his body sliding against the floor as if he was looking for a comfortable position. Something told her there wasn't one to find, not while telling this story.

"Ryan had moved to a section of the road that Echo and I had already cleared. He was continuing through to a building the commander wanted checked when the explosion hit."

Ty's hands left Kaia's back. He rubbed them over his face, through his hair and then back down again, digging his palms into his eyes in a way that made her own sting.

"God, I hated myself for weeks, thinking I'd screwed up and gotten Ryan killed." He shook his head, but didn't move his hands. "Turns out several soldiers had been hiding out inside that building, just waiting for the opportunity to strike. They'd tossed a bomb from the open windows. I just remember rock and earth exploding. Tiny shards of debris cutting into my skin, though I didn't feel the sting until much later."

His hands finally dropped back to his lap. He seemed exhausted, his normally strong features looking haggard.

"It was chaos. Men shouting. Orders flying. A cloud

of dust obscuring everything…until it cleared and I saw Ryan lying motionless on the ground. Bullets started pinging, spraying dirt. It took us a few moments to re-group, to lay cover so I could rush in and drag him out. But it was too late to save him. He was already gone."

Ty's gaze found hers for the first time since he'd started the story. The corners of his eyes tipping down with agony. A lump formed in Van's throat. She wanted to wipe it away. She'd felt that kind of pain herself, still felt it every day. She didn't want that for Ty.

He'd already suffered so much. She'd watched him struggle time and time again as they were growing up. But as a kid herself, there wasn't much she could do.

There wasn't much she could do now, either. She couldn't change the past, no matter how badly she wanted to.

"The doctors told me he most likely died on impact. He didn't know what was happening. Didn't suffer."

Reaching out, Van set her hands on either side of his face. "You're a good friend, Ty. Ryan was lucky to have you in his life."

Ty shook his head, clearly unwilling to agree with her. A few weeks ago she might have made an argument that he was right, her own pain and need to blame someone so strong. But now…she'd not only seen the undeniable goodness in the man he'd become, but she couldn't ig-nore the agony that lurked deep inside. Ty didn't deserve to carry that burden. Ryan wouldn't have wanted that.

Pushing up from the floor, he dislodged her hold. With his back to her, he said, "I'll be back in a few minutes and then we all need to try and get some sleep. It's been a long day."

He wasn't ready to listen to her. She understood that. So she'd wait until he was and then tell him again, over and over until he believed her.

9

It HAD BEEN hell to get to sleep. Not just because he was worried about Kaia, or because the floor was hard on his body. He was getting older, and his joints and muscles had no problems reminding him of that by aching. But having Van in the next room, in those little shorts that barely skimmed the lower curve of her ass and the tank top with straps so thin he could probably snap them in two seconds flat, did crazy things to his brain.

Better that than letting the memories that had unexpectedly poured out of him play over and over in his head.

He'd never meant to tell Van about that night, but for some reason, the words had simply fallen out. What surprised him most was her reaction.

He'd expected to hear her agree with him, to tell him it was all his fault that Ryan wasn't there with them.

Instead, she'd tried to give him something unexpected. Something he'd desperately needed, but didn't really deserve. Absolution.

Luckily, Kaia's nerves had been the distraction he needed. Even tucked away in the bathroom, her sensitive hearing meant every screaming rocket added to her anxiety.

Ty did the best he could, offering her comfort and a

safe place to curl up. Eventually, the fireworks died down, but Kaia was still restless. And when she did fall asleep, she was fitful, whimpering and making deep growling noises.

He'd been ready to call it a night, heading out to the couch in the den, to the blanket and pillow Van had left for him there. But the minute he'd gotten up, Kaia's nightmares got worse. So, instead, he'd grabbed the spare bedding and lain down on the floor next to Kaia.

He'd slept in a hell of a lot worse places than Van's luxurious bathroom.

The whole day had been draining. Exhaustion tugged at his body, tempting him to just give in and let everything go, at least for a little while.

And since he was safe and Kaia was okay, he did.

BARE-CHESTED, BLANKET TANGLED around his legs and one arm stretched inside Kaia's cage to rest on her back, Ty was sacked out across the cold tile floor of Van's bathroom.

The world had been a little fuzzy to her, bleary from restless sleep, until she walked into the bathroom and nearly stepped on him.

That sight could wake a girl up in a hurry.

Van stared down at him, a riot of emotions jumbling up inside her.

He looked peaceful. Until that moment, she hadn't realized the tension that constantly covered him like the blanket dipping low on his hips. But maybe she should have.

Ty always had this sense of…awareness about him. And it hadn't started when he joined the army and his office became the latest war zone. Even as a little kid, he'd always been watchful. Observant. As if he expected his environment—or the people inhabiting it—to turn on him at any moment.

The floor couldn't be that comfortable, but it obviously wasn't stopping him from sleeping. And soundly. She hadn't exactly been quiet stumbling from bed to bathroom. But he was dead to the world.

Kaia, on the other hand, had raised her head, tags jangling softly when Van entered, before dropping her head back down to rest on her paw.

She seemed a little calmer, which was a relief. Van didn't like the dog being upset.

Should she wake him and shuffle him onto the couch—or even her bed—or just leave him?

If she knew Ty at all, he wasn't likely to go back to sleep once awake. So, better to leave him where he was.

Quietly grabbing the few things she needed, Van tiptoed down to the bathroom at the opposite end of the hall, brushed her teeth, splashed water on her face and ran a brush through her hair.

Feeling a bit more alive, she headed into the kitchen for coffee. Standing at the sink, she stared out her window into the backyard.

The morning was gray, but promised to be warm and sunny with a little patience. A hushed quiet seemed to blanket the world. This was Van's favorite time of day. Sometimes she got to experience it because her life was crazy and she hadn't made it to bed yet. Sometimes she was up to get the day started early. Either way, there was something about this moment that always made her heart feel centered and light, no matter what emergency or tragedy had struck or was on the horizon.

She should rummage in the fridge and pull out something for breakfast, but she didn't. Instead, she indulged, just standing there, sipping coffee.

That's where she was, twenty minutes later, when the energy in the room changed.

She didn't need to turn to know that Ty was awake and standing behind her. She could feel him.

His presence was electric. Or maybe that was just the effect he had on her. Her skin prickled, as if he'd reached out and brushed a finger down her body.

Taking a deep breath, Van tried to find that calm that had been present just moments ago, but it had fled…as it always eventually did.

Turning, she lifted her mug to her mouth, offered him a smile around the rim and then took a sip. Swallowing, she gestured to the machine. "There's more if you want."

He didn't move, but his gaze devoured her. Trailing slowly from the tip of her head all the way down to her bare toes.

It was difficult to pull her eyes away, especially when he was standing in her kitchen, taking up more space than any man had a right to.

He hadn't bothered putting his shirt on. Not that she hadn't seen plenty of men's chests before, Ty's included, but the sight of it now made her mouth go dry. His shoulders were broad and rounded with muscle. His chest tapered down into a tight V at his hips. She knew plenty of guys who griped about their inability to gain a six-pack. Ty, despite being in his midthirties, didn't seem to have any difficulty maintaining that physique.

His jeans were well-worn and molded to his body. They looked soft and comfortable, riding low on his hips. It wouldn't take much to push her hands inside and tug them to the ground. She couldn't see a waistband. Was he going commando?

A warm rush of need washed straight to her sex.

It was too early in the morning for this. Or, rather, it was too early for her to find the will to fight her reaction.

Yanking her gaze away from him, Van turned and opened the fridge. It was a convenient barrier between them. She ducked inside, pulling out a carton of eggs, half a bell pepper, some mushrooms, cheese and ham.

Twisting, she deposited everything onto the counter by the stove. "Hope you like omeletes."

"And if I don't?"

"Then I guess you can make your own breakfast."

His mouth twisted into a grin. "Good thing I like them, then."

He didn't even bother asking, but moved right into her personal space, reaching around her to snag the pepper and mushrooms from the pile. Riffling through her drawers, he found a cutting board and knife and began to prep the veggies.

Van cracked the eggs, added some milk and a dash of black pepper. By the time she was finished, so was Ty. He had several neat piles of ingredients lined up and waiting for her.

"That was efficient," Van remarked.

Holding the handle of the knife between his thumb and forefinger, he flipped it up into the air. Van gasped and jerked backward. Ty didn't even flinch, but snatched the handle right out of the air.

"Idiot."

He tossed her an impish grin and then dropped the knife into the sink.

Van shifted to slip around him, irritation buzzing beneath

her skin. He was such a show-off. And one of these days he was going to get himself hurt with stupid, pointless stunts like that. She dealt with people in the ER every day that were there because they thought they were bulletproof… Ty was just as wrong as every last one of them; reality just hadn't caught up to him yet.

Spun up in her mental tirade, Van moved at the same time Ty did. Somehow, she ended up pinned between his big, strong body and the island in the center of her kitchen.

She gasped, the involuntary pull of air filling her lungs with the tangy, male scent of him. God, how could he smell so good after sleeping on the floor of her bathroom?

Her hands gripped the edge of the island, which was the only thing keeping them from holding him.

Not that it particularly mattered. Not when Ty's hands rested on her hips, his grasp sure and possessive. His thighs, bracketed on either side of hers, pressed into her. His chest crowded her, naked and right. There. God, she wanted to run her fingertips over him. No, her tongue. To taste his skin and feel the warmth of him filling her again.

Van's heart fluttered and her belly flip-flopped. She closed her eyes, squeezing them tight in the hopes that the moment would just pass.

But it didn't.

Instead, heat flared between them, spreading from his fingers to engulf her everywhere. Her whole body tingled.

And she wanted him. Wanted to feel something. Everything. With him. More than she'd ever wanted anything in her life.

Ty growled, a low, hungry sound that had her body throbbing.

She didn't see the kiss coming, not that it would have made a difference. It wasn't calm and easy, hardly soft and coaxing. He didn't try to win her over or convince her this was right.

He just took.

And poured passion right back into her.

His tongue laved her lips, hard and insistent. How could she refuse? Opening to him, Van dropped her head back and gave him…everything.

Tightening his grip on her hips, Ty boosted her into the air. For a few seconds she felt weightless, euphoric, until her rear landed on the cold granite countertop behind her.

Her death grip dislodged, and her hands settled on his shoulders. His skin was so warm and perfect.

"If you want me to stop you better say so now, Van." His words brushed across her skin, his mouth a ghost of temptation at the curve of her throat.

He was there with her, paused on the edge, waiting.

And, God, she wanted what he was threatening her with. The emotion. The sensation. The feeling of being alive she'd missed out on for most of her life…except for that one night with him.

Perched on the edge of her counter, Van fought the sensation of being off-kilter, his hands gripped hard around her hips the only thing preventing her from falling. But it was more, this sense of being poised either to fly or fall.

The fall scared her, but the flight pulled her in, tempted her in a way she couldn't say no to. Not anymore.

Van didn't answer him, not with words anyway. Instead, she let her fingertips skim over his skin. She traced the bold lines of the tattoos that covered his arms, shoulder and ribs. Several of them blended together, but she was too preoccupied with the man beneath the art to pay attention to what they were, what they meant. She'd ask later.

Instead, she slipped her fingers into the waistband of his jeans and tugged him closer. The hard length of his sex settled against the throbbing heat between her thighs.

Ty let out a trembling breath that ended on a groan. His hips surged against her, grinding into her. Electricity shot through Van's blood, sending a cascade of sparks down her spine.

What was it about this man that had her body responding in ways no one else had ever managed?

He ripped her soft cotton shirt over her head, flinging it across the kitchen. There was a clatter of metal against her wooden floor. Kaia's nails scrabbled against the floor as she scurried away from whatever had fallen.

Van started to push him away so she could check on the dog, but the moist heat of his mouth closing around her aching breast stopped her.

Fingers threading into his hair, she pressed him tighter against her. When had he taken her bra off? Not that it mattered. Not with the wicked edge of his tongue circling around and around, torturing her until she was breathless.

He tugged at the zipper on her shorts, never letting up on the licking, sucking, nipping pleasure he was inflicting with his mouth.

Lifting her up, Ty yanked her shorts and panties down her legs, letting them pool on the floor wherever they fell, then dropped to his knees between her spread thighs.

"Savannah," he breathed out. The way he said her name had a burst of something strong and hungry fighting through her.

With a single word he managed to make her feel beautiful, powerful and sexy. Something her previous lovers hadn't managed, and Ty wasn't even trying.

She needed her hands on him now.

Leaning forward, she gripped his arms and tried to pull him back up to her. But he refused, shaking his head.

Reaching for her, he spread the lips of her sex wide and practically dove inside. His tongue laved straight up her sex to torture her aching clit.

Van let out a cry, her head dropping back even as her body began to tremble. He sucked at her, licked and teased. Thrust his tongue deep over and over again until her hips were pushing against him, seeking more.

But it wasn't enough.

She could feel her body winding tighter and tighter, the need climbing higher and higher.

Panting, she begged, "Ty, please. I need you. Now."

With a growl and a final swirling sweep of his tongue, Ty stood. He stared down at her, his stormy-blue eyes fierce and sharp with a desire she understood because the same stinging edge was threatening to break her if he didn't give them both relief soon.

"Please," she said again.

"Condom?"

Why the hell hadn't she tucked one into the pocket of her shorts? Because she'd been living in denial, pretending there was no way this was happening again.

"Bedside table, top drawer. Hurry."

She didn't have to tell him twice. Van listened to the slap of his feet against her hard floor. Even through the sound of her own labored breaths, she could hear the squeak of the drawer in her bedroom opening and closing.

Maybe if he had been any other man, her brain might have taken those few precious moments and surfaced back to reality. Instead, the only thought running through her mind was, *hurry, hurry, hurry.*

Her body hummed, not with a gentle buzz of anticipation, but with a crackling need that threatened to consume her if she didn't find an outlet for it. Now.

Somewhere between the hall and her bedroom, Ty had lost his jeans. Pretty as you please, the man walked back into her kitchen buck naked, with his impressive erection curving long and proud.

She wanted her mouth on him. She wanted to feel the soft skin over hard steel wrapped tight in her palm as she drove him to make more of those deep growls and low hums.

His gaze was trained on her, steady and predatory. Van fought the urge to squirm against his study as he stalked toward her. His body was gorgeous, all sinewy muscle covered in beautiful art.

He hadn't bothered shaving this morning so his cheeks were covered with stubble. A shiver snaked down her spine at the memory of it scraping against her skin. And that dimple in his chin...the stubble was darker there. She wanted to run her tongue through the sexy little dip.

Pausing in front of her, his lips twisted up on one side. "Like what you see, Dr. Cantrell?"

"Now you're just fishing for compliments, soldier."

Grabbing the condom from his hand, Van tore into it and let the foil flutter down. She reached for him, pulling him closer and holding him steady so she could roll the latex over his hard shaft.

Her own sex clenched at the first feel of him.

Well, it wasn't really her first feel of him. But it was her first without her brain clouded by alcohol. She remembered enough from that night four months ago, but this morning she had perfect clarity.

Van let her hands slide up and down his cock several times. She couldn't help herself. So, maybe she was a little greedy. At the moment, no part of her regretted it.

Grasping her wrists, Ty ripped her hands away from him. She found her lips tipping down into a pout—something she never, ever did.

Ty paid her back with a hard, punishing kiss that had her body melting. The strong band of his arm around her hips brought her right to the edge of the counter. Slippery fingers played at her entrance for several seconds.

Van writhed in his arms. Whimpered. He nipped at her bottom lip, tugging it into his mouth and sucking as two fingers sank deep inside her.

Her hips surged against him, wanting, seeking more.

"Not enough," she breathed out.

Digging her heels into the backs of his thighs, Van reached between them and found him. She could feel the pulse of his heartbeat, fast and heavy, through the skin covering his erection. Felt the same relentless rhythm beating deep inside her own body.

Spreading her thighs wide, she guided him where she wanted him and felt relief when the head of his cock nudged against her entrance.

"Now, God, now."

With one quick thrust, Ty slid deep. The friction felt fabulous and perfect. Exactly what she needed, only it wasn't enough. Not yet.

"More."

"Greedy little thing," he gritted out between clenched teeth. But gave her exactly what she wanted, pulling out and slowly thrusting back in again.

Slow and steady at first, Ty gave her a cadence that drove her higher and higher. Pleasure flowed from him to her and back again, blazing hot and building more with each passing moment.

Van's own hips bucked against his, unable to stay still as she fought for each blinding moment they shared together. She needed it. Needed this. Needed him.

Her entire body quivered, so close to an explosion she knew was going to leave her mindless, breathless, shattered. It scared her just as much as she fought for it.

"Give it to me, Van. I've got you. I promise, princess."

His words, whispered so gently against her temple, were her undoing.

The orgasm crashed over her like a twenty-foot wave, stealing all her oxygen and sucking her into the swirling tempest of sensation.

All she knew was that she clung to him, the solid form of his body the only sure thing in the world at that moment.

Her name was a muffled cry as he buried his face into the cloud of her messy hair. His own body shuddered even as his hips pistoned with several deep strokes before going still between her spread thighs.

Their skin was damp and slick. Van's lungs stuttered with every breath, almost like they'd forgotten how to function. She groaned a little when she shifted, the backs of her thighs rubbed raw against the stone countertop she still sat on.

She could feel him, buried deep inside her. She was pinned in place by the heavy weight of his body.

And that sent a curl of panic through her chest.

Because it wasn't just physical. She could have taken a palm and shoved him off her. Did, actually, taking in the sleepy, satisfied way Ty blinked at her through his narrowed gaze.

She was suffocating. Needed space.

Jumping off the counter, she scooped her shorts up off the floor, strode over to where her shirt and bra sat covered by a pile of perfectly chopped peppers and mushrooms.

"I'm taking a shower."

Before he could react, Van shot into her bedroom, shut the door behind her and turned the lock for good measure.

Dropping down into a crouch in the middle of the room, she clutched the pile of clothes to her chest and bowed her head.

Shit.

10

VAN GROANED AND rolled over. It took her several seconds to realize what had pulled her from the restless sleep she'd finally fallen into.

Her phone buzzed on the nightstand, the screen glowing bright in the dark.

Calls this early were never good.

Ty, her parents—if something had happened to them...

Wide awake now, she snatched the phone up and answered in a rush. "Yes?"

"Van, I'm so sorry to call this early." All the fear and energy rushed out of her at the sound of her boss's voice. Stifling another groan, Van flopped back onto the bed and squeezed her eyes shut.

Clearly, no one she cared about had been in a horrible accident—and she wasn't ready to contemplate why Ty had come first in the list of people to worry about—but that didn't mean this call was going to be good. In fact, it was going to be very bad.

"I know you're supposed to be on vacation until the middle of next week—"

"The first vacation time I've taken in two years." Not counting the time she'd taken off for Ryan's funeral, which definitely wasn't a vacation.

"I know. But a stomach virus has hit the hospital and I'm severely short-staffed. I could really use the help. Ten hours. That's all I need. I promise."

This is what she got for staying home during her time off instead of slipping away to some mountain retreat. Quiet nights full of clear skies and stars so big they felt close enough to touch. Cool, crisp mountain air. Long hikes, just her and her thoughts. Van closed her eyes and could practically feel the sun warming her skin.

"Van?"

"What?"

"Seriously. You know I wouldn't call if I didn't really need you."

With a sigh, she pushed up from the bed. Tina was a damn good chief of staff for the hospital. She'd been a friend and mentor long before she'd become her boss. And Tina was right; she knew how much Van had needed a break from the hospital, from her life, from all the pain and grief of the last few months. She wouldn't have called if she had another option.

"Fine. I'll be there in an hour. But I don't care what's going on, when that clock hits six p.m. I'm out the door. You better start figuring out which sucker you're going to call in for the evening shift."

Tina chuckled. "That sucker's already lined up."

"Perfect."

Rolling out of bed, Van fell into her normal routine. Maybe it was a good thing she was going in. Several hours of high-pressured work would at least keep her brain from spinning back to amazing kitchen-counter sex.

And how much she really wanted to do it again.

Even if that would be the stupidest move she'd ever made.

Or maybe the stupidest move she'd ever made was letting Ty Colson spend the night on her bathroom floor in the first place.

Memories assaulted her, revving her body and making parts of it throb with banked need. Their first time together had left fuzzy impressions. Good ones that had tortured her in her dreams.

But yesterday…without the numbing edge of alcohol every last detail of her romp with Ty was etched into her brain. God, the man approached sex just like everything else in his life—full throttle.

Ty was reckless and always had been. She couldn't handle reckless. Not and keep her sanity intact.

It was so tempting, though, like that college friend offering a smoldering joint in the middle of a party and promising you one hit won't ruin your life. Maybe not, but the likelihood was one hit would never be enough.

She already knew that adage was true of Ty. One night with him would never be enough. But she couldn't have more.

Couldn't allow herself to have more.

The problem was, she could see herself so easily falling for the man. Hell, she was already half in love with him and had been since she was a little girl. The guy was larger than life. People were drawn to his charm, brash personality and the sense of honor that he wore like a badge.

But letting herself go there would only end in heartache. At the end of the day, Ty would leave. And not just leave, but go back to a place so dangerous people came home in body bags.

She confronted death every day. Waged war against it, and thankfully won, more times than not. But she was realistic enough to understand that no doctor—not even the best-trained ones—could save everyone. Hell, her brother was the perfect example of that. Dead probably before his body hit the ground.

In the ER, she swooped in, patched them up and sent them on to their next destination. She spent minutes with her patients, never enough time to really connect with them.

Not that she particularly minded. In fact in her opinion, that disconnect made her better at her job. It allowed her to look past emotions to what would save a life. She didn't agonize over her decisions; she rarely had the luxury of that kind of time. Not in those life-or-death moments.

So what was it about Ty Colson that had her agonizing over everything?

At least work would provide a distraction.

In fact, walking into the chaos, it was clear she wouldn't have time for much of anything except focusing on the patients in front of her. No phone calls or texts in a moment of weakness. No wondering what he was doing or whether he was thinking about her and what they'd done.

Nope, just blood, crisis and the adrenaline that spiked during those moments.

Stowing her stuff, she walked onto the floor and grabbed the chart for her first patient.

Twelve hours later, she realized the plan had worked. She'd stayed long past her shift, unable to leave when the ER was slammed and understaffed. And hadn't thought of Ty once. But her body ached, her eyes were gritty from her restless night before and her stomach grumbled since she hadn't had time to eat.

"Incoming. Car accident. Unconscious on scene and hasn't come around. Minute and a half."

Van grabbed the bottle of water she'd set on the nurse's station, and chugged it back.

Red lights flashed across the large glass doors. They opened with a silent whoosh as her nursing staff rushed out to greet the ambulance.

When had it gotten dark? And when had it started to rain?

Shaking her head, Van followed at a trot. Around her, nurses gathered information from the paramedics and relayed it to her and the rest of the team.

She reached the cluster of people running alongside the man strapped to the gurney.

People were calling out details. "SUV hit a tree head-on." The words registered even as Van's gaze began visually assessing the patient from his feet up. They sped through the halls toward trauma two.

"Airbag deployed. Wearing his seat belt."

For some reason her stomach rolled when she reached the man's hands. Electricity zinged up her spine and felt like it exploded out the back of her head.

"Unconscious on the scene and still hasn't come around."

She didn't understand why until her gaze came to rest on his face.

"Shit," she said, grinding to a halt.

Behind her, Cara, a nurse who'd been with the hospital for almost twenty years, slammed into her back. "Van? What's wrong?"

Her throat tightened, but she forced the words out anyway. "I know him."

Cara just stared at her expectantly.

Van looked down at her, panic welling inside her chest. "I *know* him," she said again, unconsciously putting emphasis on the second word.

Cara's eyes widened. "Oh."

It was against hospital policy to treat anyone you were involved with. She should call for another doctor.

A loud, low groan came from the gurney, now several feet ahead of them. From where she stood, Van watched Ty rear up, or try to, and begin to thrash against the straps holding him down.

Possessiveness jolted through her. There was no way she was letting anyone else touch him. Ty needed her and that was all that mattered.

Shaking Cara's hand off, she rushed into the large room Ty and her team had disappeared into.

Edging a nurse out of the way, Van positioned herself right next to Ty's head. Placing a hand on his forehead, she forced him to lie back down. If he'd hurt his spine or neck he was only going to do more damage. She'd protect him, even from himself.

His eyes were open, but they were unfocused and glazed.

"Ty," she said softly.

"Stop" he growled, his voice trailing to a moan. "That hurts." Suddenly, he started thrashing, fighting against the straps holding him down and screaming. "No. Don't touch me!"

Someone behind her gasped, but Van didn't have time to deal with anyone else's reaction. Or the sick sensation that settled into her own belly as she realized Ty was stuck inside a terrible memory. And, knowing him, he'd be mortified to learn of the public display.

Leaning close, Van placed her mouth at Ty's ear. "Ty,

it's me, Van." His body stilled, the straining muscles relaxing against the straps holding him in place. So she continued. "No one's going to hurt you. You've been in a car accident. You're strapped down to prevent you from further injuring yourself until we assess the damage."

She pulled away several inches, enough that she could look into his eyes again. This time, his stormy-blue gaze was clear, though sharp with the edge of pain.

"Van?"

Her fingers smoothed over his forehead, shifting strands of hair away from his face. "Yeah."

"Where's Kaia?"

Oh, hell.

"What do you mean?"

"Your parents asked me to check on her since you were at work. I picked her up and we were out driving. The rain came down fast. We must have hydroplaned."

Shit. Kaia had been in the car?

Ty began to struggle against the bindings again, his hands fruitlessly trying to free himself. "I have to find her."

Glancing up, Van caught the eye of a nurse standing at the back of the room. "He had a dog with him. Kaia. She's a retired military dog who lost a leg overseas. Please find out what you can from the paramedics."

She turned to Ty. "We'll figure out where she is, Ty. I promise. But right now I need you to lie still so we can assess how you're doing."

"No. I'm fine. A few bumps and scratches."

"The paramedics said you were unconscious when they found you, and you only just came to. That's not a great sign, Ty. At the very least we need a CAT scan to

make sure you don't have a more extensive brain injury
or internal bleeding."

"I'm fine," he said again, through clenched teeth.

Stubborn man. "You might be fine, but I'm not letting
you up until I verify that with medical technology, so you
might as well lie still and enjoy the attention."

Pulling out a pen light, Van placed a hand on his forehead and shined it straight into his eyes. He flinched and
squeezed them shut. "Goddammit, Van. Warn a guy."

"I'm going to shine a bright light in your eyes, you
big baby. Better?"

The nurse rushed back in. Leaning close she said,
"One of the paramedics said the dog was at the scene. A
firefighter has her. They're bringing her here."

Van thanked the young nurse with a smile before turning back to Ty. "There. Now you can stop worrying and
start letting me do my job. The faster I get all these tests
done the sooner you can walk out the door."

"Fine," Ty grumbled, his body finally going lax
against the spinal board beneath him.

Van didn't miss his minuscule wince or the flash of
pain that crossed his face. It did little to settle the anxiety that made her heart stutter uncomfortably.

She couldn't do anything about that. But she did have
the knowledge and experience to handle Ty's injuries.
That was a problem she could tackle.

TY WAS DONE with this place. It was almost midnight, and
if it weren't for Van he would have left a long time ago.
But each time he got ready to, he'd see the flash of fear
cross her face.

On one hand it bothered him that she felt it at all.

On the other, it meant that she cared, right? Something

he wasn't entirely certain of after the way she'd walked out on him yesterday.

Not that he had a reputation of love 'em and leave 'em, but Ty was used to being the one hoping to extricate himself after a sexual encounter.

It hadn't felt great having the shoe on the other foot.

Especially when Van was involved.

What he'd really wanted to do was scoop her into his arms, find the nearest bed and spend the rest of the day there, waking up whenever the mood struck him to love her again.

Instead, his brain had barely been engaged when she'd pushed away from him, scooped up her clothes and locked herself behind that bedroom door. She'd moved so fast Ty didn't even have time to react.

Or stop her.

Standing in the middle of her kitchen, staring dumbfounded after her, had left a bitter taste in his mouth. Especially considering how wholly their encounter had rocked his foundations.

He'd had two choices, wait her out—eventually she'd have to leave that room—or go, give her the space she apparently needed, and come back later to tackle whatever had sent her scurrying away like he'd sprouted a forked tongue and tail.

A prudent soldier always recognized when it was smart to retreat and regroup, so he'd left, his body still humming from the best orgasm of his life.

He'd still been stewing when he'd gotten the call from Margaret asking him to swing by and check on Kaia since Van had been called in to the hospital.

"How did you get into my house anyway?"

Van busied herself with something at the counter on

the other side of the room, clinking together instruments and bottles, or whatever.

Surely, she had things she needed to do, but she'd pretty much been in his room since the moment they wheeled him in. In a different situation he might have assumed that meant she couldn't bring herself to move away from him.

In reality, he was pretty sure she was afraid he'd walk out the door the minute she turned her back.

She wasn't wrong. The thought had crossed his mind. More than once.

"Your mom gave me a key."

Van's mouth twitched and then pulled into a frown. "Remind me to yell at her for that."

"You know that's not going to happen." A smirk twisted his lips but didn't stay long. "Have you seen Kaia? Is she okay?"

That, more than anything, was what worried him right now. "She's been through so much already. She might be masking the pain of any injuries because she's worried about me. She's like that. Loyal."

Van glanced at him over her shoulder, her deep green eyes a mix of emotions—understanding, gratitude, the dull ache of a quiet pain. "I'm aware. I called in a favor from a friend. She's been looked at by a vet and cleared. She's outside because security won't let her in."

Ty grumbled beneath his breath. He understood this wasn't a war zone where Kaia could have free rein, but it wasn't like she was some random puppy without training or discipline.

"I should have told them she was my Seeing Eye dog."

Van laughed, the sound a little ragged at the edges.

"Yeah, that would have made things easier for the cop writing up your accident."

He grimaced and then winced when the movement made his head pound.

Van was across the room like a shot, her soft, warm hand pressed against his forehead, tipping it back. Her gaze bounced back and forth between his eyes, no doubt looking for signs that he was harboring some internal time bomb waiting to explode.

"Chill out, princess. I'm fine."

"You say that, but it's not true. You were unconscious for quite a while. That's not nothing, Ty."

"Maybe I didn't have anything to wake up for until I heard your voice."

Shit. He hadn't meant to say those words out loud.

He expected her to pull away, like she'd done yesterday when things got too intense. But she didn't. Instead, Van simply stared at him, her eyes wide and troubled.

"You can't say things like that."

Screw it. Tiptoeing around her wasn't going to get him anywhere. Van was the kind of woman who understood action.

"Why not? It's the truth. I've wanted you for years, Savannah. I'm done pretending that's not true, or telling myself I'm not good enough for you or that I need to leave you alone because you're Ryan's sister. The last few months have been hell, but they've taught me one thing. Life is too precious to not live it wide open."

An unhappy sound rumbled through Van's chest, a cross between a laugh and a wheeze.

"I'm pretty sure you've always lived your life that way, Ty. Nothing new about your philosophy now. It's something I envy about you." There was a slight hitch to her words. "You don't apologize or pull punches. You do what you want, what needs to be done…no matter the consequences."

"That doesn't sound good, Van. Not when you say it in that murky, dejected tone of voice."

She shook her head, dark hair flying around her face. "Doing the right thing is always good. Even when it's not the easy thing." Her hand slipped down his forehead to settle against the curve of his cheek. "And what's this bullshit about you not being good enough for me? You're a war hero. I'm pretty sure that makes you good enough for anyone you want. There's currently a cluster of nurses lingering outside your door just waiting for the chance to take your temperature or fetch you water."

"Why, doctor, is that jealousy I hear?"

Van's eyes widened, deliberately. She stared at him out of that deep green gaze that always had the ability to slice right through him. "I'm sure I don't know what you're talking about."

But she couldn't stop the twitch of humor at the edge of her lips.

Ty felt an answering laugh bubble up inside his chest. Without a thought to what he was actually doing, he wrapped a hand around the nape of her neck and pulled her close. "You. I want you." His words were husky.

That sweet, spicy scent of hers swirled around him, filling his lungs and making his body ache in ways that had nothing to do with his accident. Her skin was soft beneath his fingers. The silky strands of her hair brushed against the back of his hand. Even those few simple touches had his body reacting.

The accident clearly hadn't injured his dick, since it was currently tenting the gown Van's staff had slipped him into after cutting the clothes from his body. A shame since he'd really liked the jeans he'd been wearing. They were worn in and comfortable as hell.

Van's eyes closed. Her head bowed until her forehead pressed against his. Ty slid his hands to her waist, bracketing her hips and fighting the urge to pull her down onto the bed with him so he could feel her next to him.

Not the time. Not the place.

Instead, he just breathed her in. Pulled her deep into his lungs and held her there. Appreciated the warmth radiating from her body and soaking deep beneath his skin.

He couldn't remember the last time he'd felt like this. Warm. Cared for. Safe. Ty was used to being the one to provide those things. He'd never really been given them.

Ty had no idea how long they stood like that. Long enough for him to realize she hadn't responded to the bold statement he'd made, at least not with words. And her actions weren't exactly clear-cut, either.

But she hadn't walked away.

Behind them, someone cleared their throat. "Sorry to interrupt, Dr. Cantrell, but the results are back."

At the first sound, Van sprang away, looking more like a guilty teenager caught with her hand down his pants than a seasoned ER doctor who'd been innocently touching him. The blush that stained her cheeks didn't help alleviate the impression.

Ty liked it. He liked seeing her a little flustered. The color on her skin made her look…innocent, a word he never would have thought to use to describe Van. Because she wasn't. But the reaction was sweet.

The nurse hovering in the doorway apparently thought so as well if the grin spreading across her face was any indication.

"No problem, Cara. Let's take a look."

Her mantle of authority firmly back in place, Van went to powwow with the nurse in the corner. She flipped through a couple papers on his chart, a tiny frown puckering the skin right between her eyes. He wasn't sure if that was concentration or concern.

No matter. She'd tell him soon enough. Aside from a massive headache, he really did feel fine.

"Well, all of your blood tests returned normal and your CAT scan is clear, but you definitely have a concussion. I'd like to keep you here overnight for observation."

No way in hell. "That's a little extreme, don't you think, Van?"

"What is it you guys say? Standard operating procedure?"

"So you're telling me that every patient who comes into the ER with nothing more than a concussion gets admitted for observation?"

He might have thought the scowl that pinched her face was funny if they weren't currently talking about his freedom for the next several hours. He wanted out and needed to check on Kaia. Despite Van's assurances that she was okay, he wouldn't be satisfied until he'd checked her over himself.

"They do if they were unconscious at the scene of a car accident." Van's scowl deepened.

"Don't make me check myself out AMA, Van," he countered.

The bullish expression on her face told him he was in for an argument.

Until Cara, his new best friend, spoke up. "Van, it's not unheard of to release a concussion patient into someone else's care, with instructions on what complications to look for."

Ty shifted up so that he could throw Cara a huge smile to counteract the glare Van shot in her direction. "The problem is, you don't have anyone to follow the proper protocol," Van ground out between clenched teeth.

"Sure I do."

Her gaze narrowed and the jealousy that had amused him several minutes ago flashed sharp and deep in her eyes.

Ty crossed his arms over his chest, enjoying the way her gaze strayed to the bulge of his biceps against the cuff of the gown. Just because he could, he flexed the muscles again. Van's frown deepened and her green eyes jerked back to his face.

"Who?"

"You."

Her mouth opened and then shut without a single word coming out. Behind them, Cara smothered a snicker, though not very well.

"Nope. I have to work."

"Tina asked me to remind you that you're off the clock," Cara said. "Technically, Ty's care has already been shifted to Dr. Brighton. She also wanted me to remind you that ten hours was almost six hours ago and that she's not to see you inside that door for the next five days."

Savannah let out a strangled sound, somewhere between a harrumph and a groan. Her eyes smoldered with irritation and her arms crossed over her chest. No doubt, she was completely unaware of how the pose pushed her breasts against the tight fabric of her scrubs. "Sure, seventeen hours ago she was begging me to come in because she didn't have another choice," she grumbled beneath her breath.

Ty didn't even bother suppressing his chuckle. "It would appear you're free to nurse me back to health, Dr. Cantrell. Just my luck."

Spinning on her heel, she stomped toward the door. Ty enjoyed the way her white lab coat swirled out around her body. She didn't slow down, tossing orders at Cara as she passed. "Prepare his discharge papers."

"Where are you going?" Ty pushed up onto his elbows—to get a better view of her stormy exit—and yelled after her. But she didn't pause or respond.

Cara leaned against the door jamb. "Whatever you're doing, keep doing it. I've never seen her like this."

"You mean pissed off? I know Van. That can't be true."

"Oh, no, I've seen her pissed off plenty. I've never seen her this flustered, by anyone or anything." She straightened, and pinned him beneath the sharp cut of her gaze. "Do not screw this up, buddy. You might be a tough military man, but I will hunt you down and hurt you."

"Yes, ma'am," Ty said, fighting to keep the grin from breaking across his face.

With a single, sharp nod of her head, Cara disappeared into the hallway.

11

TY LET HIS head fall back onto the raised bed behind him. His skull felt like the seven dwarfs were taking their pickaxes to his brain. The room was a little wonky as well, something he hadn't mentioned to Van. So, he had a concussion. He'd had them before. The rest of his body was a little sore, and no doubt he'd feel the impact even more tomorrow.

The silence was pleasant, especially after the chaos he'd woken up to as they'd rolled him into the ER. Exhaustion pulled at him, but a quiet click announced the opening and closing of the door to the room. Ty couldn't bring himself to open his eyes. Until the telltale sound of tags jingled. A heavy weight landed on the edge of the bed, jolting him and making him wince. When he opened his eyes it was to see Kaia, her front paw next to his hip, staring at him with those warm brown eyes. Her mouth was open and her tongue lolled out in an expression that was nothing short of a doggy grin.

Van hovered behind her.

"I thought security wouldn't let her through."

She shrugged. "What good is being a doctor if it doesn't come with a few perks? I told them she was your service dog for PTSD."

"Clever."

"Besides, when I went out to check on her, she looked about as good as you did when you first arrived."

Ty shifted up higher against the bed and placed his hands on Kaia's head. Concern tinged his voice when he asked, "You okay, girl?"

"She's fine. The vet looked at her, although she wasn't very cooperative with the exam."

"You've had your fill of doctors, haven't you?" Ty scratched behind her ears just the way she liked. "I'm starting to feel that way myself. Well, except for one pretty amazing exception."

Ty grinned, glancing at Van out of the corner of his eyes.

He liked the way she shifted and a blush slowly spread into her cheeks. Not to mention the way she pointedly ignored what he'd just said.

"He had a hell of a time getting her away from the front doors. Security said she tried to dart in several times when they opened. The fireman who brought her over from the scene finally found a length of rope and tied her to a bike rack."

An involuntary growl rumbled through Ty's chest.

"Easy, soldier," Van said, moving closer and resting a soothing hand on his shoulder. "He stayed right by her side. He was worried she was going to get caught as the doors closed."

Yeah, he got it. But still…

"Kaia pulled the rope as far as it would go, plopped down on her rear and stayed right there with her gaze trained on the activity inside for the past several hours. She wouldn't eat or drink. She just wanted to make sure you were okay."

Van's fingers tightened on his shoulder for a second, warmth rolling over his body from the touch. But then she backed off, letting her arm drop to her side.

"All that's to say my little white lie wasn't really for you. It was for her."

"Whatever you want to tell yourself, princess."

Van opened her mouth to argue; the hard, determined light in her eyes clearly telegraphed that intention. But she didn't get the chance.

Cara pushed open the door. "Okay, you're all set. Normally, I'd provide your caregiver with information about your condition, but I'm pretty sure Van has that well in hand." The petite blonde flashed a knowing smile at them both. "You're free to go."

WHAT THE HELL was she supposed to do with him now? She couldn't send him back to his hotel, not with a clear conscience. But the last time they were together at her place proved close proximity to Ty Colson was not her friend.

At least not if she had any hope of protecting herself from a major dose of heartache.

Glancing over at him in the passenger seat, Van realized it was probably way too late to worry about that.

The fear that had overwhelmed her—frozen her—when she'd realized he was the patient unconscious on that gurney was a sensation she never wanted to experience again.

She'd heard horror stories of ER doctors being presented with their own loved ones as patients, but had never experienced it herself. Over the last several months there'd been a part of her that was angry she hadn't been there to help Ryan. If only she'd been by his side, could she have saved him?

She'd read the medical report and logically understood that wasn't likely. His internal injuries were too severe. She had no doubt he'd died on impact.

But she was enough of a control freak that it was difficult to let that possibility go, because she hadn't had the chance.

Today had given her a small dose of what that experience would have been like, and she didn't like it.

Even now, after seeing Ty's tests, studying his scans and knowing he had no major complications from the accident, she still couldn't shake the fear he was going to drop from some injury she'd missed.

Shaking off the anxious thought, she said, "I suppose this blows your plans for some time on the beach."

Ty rolled his head against the rest, his blue-gray gaze studying her for several seconds. "That depends on you. As I understand it, you're off for the next five days. Care to visit somewhere tropical and sandy with me?"

"Not really."

Ty frowned. Clearly, that wasn't the answer he'd expected. "Really?"

"I hate sand. It gets into everything and chafes like a son of a bitch. I refuse to get in the water. Seaweed and little fishies nibbling at my feet." Van gave an involuntary shudder. "Enough said. Not to mention that I burn after fifteen minutes in the sun."

"Maybe you wouldn't burn if instead of working fourteen-hour days, you actually ventured into the daylight once in a while."

"Oh, like you're so clever. You work in the desert and are surrounded by sand all the time—why on God's green earth would you want to spend your vacation at the beach?"

Ty rolled his eyes. "Fine. No beach. So where do you like to go when you have time off?"

"I don't know. I haven't taken a vacation in several years." Van's gaze darted around. "Actually, I was thinking about heading over to Colorado and renting a cabin in the mountains."

"Sold."

Her startled eyes jerked to his. "Wait. What?"

"Let's do that. Our options are to spend the next couple days cooped up in your house or spend them in a luxurious cabin overlooking the gorgeous vista of the Rocky Mountains. I know which one I'd prefer."

"Just like that?"

Ty reached over and grabbed her hand. Instinct told her she should pull away, but she couldn't make herself do it. Not when his touch felt so good.

Comforting and safe. Warm and alive.

"Just like that. You need a lot more spontaneity in your life, Van."

She grimaced, mostly because he wasn't wrong. Although she was loath to admit it...especially to him. "And I suppose you think you're just the person to show me the light?"

He shrugged, the movement of his wide shoulders catching her gaze. Van had no doubt those shoulders could hold the weight of the world if needed. Ty wasn't just strong, but capable, direct and authoritative, with enough of a dash of unpredictable to make life interesting.

Why the hell was she trying to avoid him?

Oh, yeah, because at the end of these five days he was

going to leave and return to a war zone that had already cost her one person she loved.

Van stared into Ty's gaze. God, she wanted to say yes. Desperately. There was nothing right now she wanted more than a few days of secluded bliss with this man. There was no doubt he'd rock her world. He'd already done it twice.

But it was more than that. More than just stellar sex.

There was something about Ty that...centered her, even as his nearness distracted and aroused her. When he was around, the edge of restlessness that she constantly struggled with, and normally combatted with work, simply disappeared.

Was it so wrong to want that, even if she could only have it for a little while?

As if sensing her internal struggle, Ty reached out. The backs of his fingers slowly slid down the curve of her cheek, his thumb grazing the line of her jaw, coaxing without saying a single word.

He suddenly looked so serious. She could see the darkness in his gaze, lurking beneath the surface. And just like she'd been desperate to fix him in the ER, she felt an overwhelming urge to make it right.

But she was smart enough to realize she couldn't. Nothing could erase the things he'd seen and done.

Van swallowed and whispered, "Okay."

Ty's lips quirked up on one side. His gaze narrowed and a promising smolder replaced that darkness.

Uh-oh.

"I'll make a couple calls while you pack." Clearly in go mode, Ty bounded from the car as if he hadn't just spent several hours in the ER.

Men.

Holding the door open for Kaia, Van watched her jump to the ground and follow Ty onto the porch, moving much slower than he had. She didn't blame the dog. It was after midnight. Van had been at the hospital for hours and the exhaustion she'd been holding back with sheer will was threatening to finally win.

Letting out a stream of air that fluttered her bangs, Van was already regretting her decision as she followed. Plopping down into one of the rockers on her front porch, Ty pulled his cell from a pocket and began punching buttons.

"Don't forget to pack Kaia's things," he said, pausing midpunch. "I'll grab her crate. If we get on the road in the next hour we could get there by late afternoon."

Stalking across the porch, Van didn't pause as she crowded into his personal space and snatched the phone out of Ty's hand.

"Hey," he said, hands chasing after it as she slipped it behind her back.

Van hadn't realized she'd walked straight between his open thighs until Ty's chest collided with her torso. His hands wrapped around her hips and a cocky grin twisted his lips.

He stared up at her. She had a flashback of that same damn expression when he had her spread out on the kitchen island. Heat slammed through her, stealing her breath for a few seconds.

Nope. That wasn't what she'd come over here to do.

"First, if this is a vacation then you need to look up the definition of the word. I will not rush through packing and forget half of what I actually need because you didn't give me adequate time to prepare."

The grin on Ty's face got wider, which only made Van's eyes narrow.

"Princess, if you forget anything, I'll buy it for you."

"That's stupid, Ty. We have plenty of time."

"Not if we want to get to Colorado as soon as possible."

She shook her head. "Isn't happening. I haven't slept in about fourteen hours. I can't pick up and drive for another twelve just because you've suddenly got a burr up your ass."

"So sleep while I drive."

"Not a snowball's chance in hell. You were just released from the ER with a concussion. Do you really think I'm going to let you drive? Let alone fall asleep while you do it?"

"I'm fine, Van."

Even as he said the words, an aftershock of fear slammed through her. Several hours ago, he hadn't looked fine at all. Her body locked and her jaw clamped tight.

He must have recognized the signs, because his expression gentled and his hold on her tightened.

"I'm fine, Van. I promise."

She snorted. "That's not what your doctor diagnosed. She's pretty damn smart and absolutely certain you have a concussion. So, unless you plan on going to Colorado alone, I suggest you temper your enthusiasm, soldier. Make your calls, find us a cabin and we'll leave in the morning."

Ty grumbled, but he didn't argue.

Instead, he surged up from the rocker, taking her with him. Van squealed, her arms and legs automatically wrapping around his body.

Taking the keys from her fingers, he unlocked the

door and ushered Kaia into the house ahead of them, all without dropping Van. There was a part of her that was impressed.

Ty kicked the door shut behind them and headed for the back of the house.

"What are you doing?" she asked, squirming in his hold.

"Taking you to bed." His mouth landed on her neck, trailing open-mouthed kisses along her skin and leaving a line of fire in his wake. "We've had drunken sex in our childhood playhouse and amazing counter sex before you freaked and kicked me out of your house."

"I did *not* freak."

He raised a single eyebrow, silently calling her on her bullshit.

"Fine. I freaked. A little. We're crossing lines here, Ty. Lines I'd planned on keeping clear and unbroken."

Shaking his head, Ty bent down and found her mouth. He kissed her, deep and thorough, pushing every ounce of his desire for her into the connection.

"Too late," he whispered against her lips. "Those lines have been blurred for a very long time."

He could see the struggle in her gaze as she tried to convince herself to push him away. And he wasn't opposed to using guerrilla warfare when it was required. Finding the pulse at the base of her throat, Ty licked it and then sucked.

She couldn't hold back a moan. The sound went straight to his dick, making it throb.

"You have a concussion," she breathed, her voice low and wavering, throbbing with the desire he created. Striding down the hall with her wrapped around his body,

Ty gave her a wicked grin. "Consider this my follow-up exam, doc."

She laughed, the sound hitching when he shifted her in his arms, his fingers finding the curve of her thigh and following up to caress her center.

The dampness he found there had something primitive roaring through his blood. He'd caused that. He'd aroused her to that point. God, he wanted to taste her. To put his tongue right there and feel her overwhelming heat.

Dropping her onto the bed, Ty followed her down. He ripped at her clothes, buttons, zippers, straps and clasps. They all stood in the way of seeing her. Feeling her.

She didn't protest. Instead, she did the same. Plucking at his own clothes. They grunted with the effort, then laughed when the tight neck of his shirt got stuck half on and half off over his head.

Her mischievous playfulness was such a contrast to the capable and efficient doctor who'd stayed by his side for the last several hours. He could appreciate how good she was at her job, but that wasn't a surprise. Van succeeded at anything she put her mind to.

But this was a side Ty knew not many got to see. Even growing up, Van had rarely opened up enough to feel comfortable being her true self. But she'd done it with him back then. And now she was sharing that gift again.

He wanted more.

He wanted everything.

With impatient hands, Ty tore the shirt over his head, uncaring at the ripping sound of seams giving way. Whatever. He'd replace it.

Finally naked, Ty leaned down and wrapped an arm beneath Savannah's waist. He pulled her up, scooted her to the center of the bed and stood back so he could simply look at her.

A flush swept across her skin, a gorgeous glow of pink that made her skin appear almost luminous in the darkened room. Neither of them had bothered to flip on a switch or open the curtains.

She shifted, her gaze drifting away from his, and he realized she was uncomfortable with him watching her.

And that seemed so wrong.

"Do you have any idea how breathtaking you are, Savannah Cantrell?

Her eyes, bright green, swung back to his. He could read the uncertainty there and wanted to kick any man's ass who'd been in her life and hadn't reinforced that single truth.

"I see you. All of you. And I don't just mean your body. I *know* you. You're physically beautiful, any man's wet dream. But you're more than that, Van. You're intelligent, dedicated, loyal and honest. You put others before yourself time and time again, expecting nothing in return. Trust me when I say you're breathtaking."

"Okay." She said the word, but he could see she still didn't completely believe him.

Didn't matter. There was another, more pleasurable way to convince her.

Placing a knee on the bed between her open thighs, Ty crawled toward her. Her eyes flared and then narrowed, want kindling deep inside.

Yes.

Placing a hand on her calf, he let his fingers slowly slide up. She shifted, restless beneath the simple caress. She wanted more. So did he.

His other hand settled on her thigh, pushing gently

until she spread open for him. The scent of her arousal bloomed around him, musk and sex and desire.

She reached for him, clearly still uneasy over the attention.

Grasping her hand, Ty set it gently on the bed beside her. "Nope. You get to enjoy. Take what I'm giving you, Van. Take it all. I want you to feel how beautiful you are. Understand that to me, every inch of you is fascinating and inspiring."

Her fingers tightened on the sheet at her hip, digging into the mattress beneath the cloth. Her hips shifted, rising off the bed as her back arched.

A grin tugged at his lips.

"Cocky bastard," she breathed out, even as she silently begged for more.

"Guilty as charged." But that wasn't going to stop him. And she knew it.

Ty's fingers slipped across her skin, up her legs, over her ribs, across her belly, collarbone. The ball of her shoulder and each slender finger on her hands. He caressed and teased. Kneading into her muscles and then barely skimming across her skin, forcing goose bumps to the surface.

The dark pink tips of her breasts puckered, begging him, but he ignored them. When his palm grazed close to the strip of hair covering her sex, Van whimpered. But he ignored that pretty plea, too.

He wasn't satisfied until she was writhing, her body following the path of each caress, bucking and pushing into him, searching for more.

Her eyes gleamed with need, with desire and impatience.

"Stop teasing me, Ty. You've made your point."

"Have I?"

"Yes. Now for the love of all that's good and holy, touch me."

"Pretty sure that's what I've been doing, princess."

Her gaze narrowed. She took a deep breath, her breasts bobbing with the motion. God, he wasn't going to last much longer. She wasn't the only one he'd been torturing all this time.

His cock was so hard the ache was an incessant beat pounding through his body.

"Screw this." Van surged up, grasped his shoulders in both hands and twisted.

He was surprised, and still off his game from the concussion—that was the only reason she got the jump on him. Even as his back hit the bed, Ty blinked up at her in astonishment.

But Van was a woman on a mission.

Straddling his hips, she pinned him down with the weight of her body. Even so, he could have had their positions flipped in seconds flat. But he wanted to see what she'd do; Savannah Cantrell in charge was a sexy thing to behold.

Dark brown hair swirled around her shoulders, tumbling down her back. She leaned over him, bringing the pouting tip of her nipple close enough for him to surge up and suck it deep inside.

She groaned, her hips rolling against him. Her slick arousal spread across his pulsing erection.

"Now touch me," she panted, demanding, "like you mean it."

Scraping his teeth lightly over her skin, he dragged them up until he gently held the tight bud between his teeth. He sucked in air, letting it slip across her wet skin and then flicked at the tip he held prisoner.

"Freaking hell," she groaned, even as she fumbled inside the bedside table. He knew exactly what she was going for and decided to see just how distracted he could make her.

Pushing his hips deep into the bed, he slipped a hand between them and found her slick center. Sinking his fingers deep inside was heaven.

She was so hot and wet. The muscles of her sex clamped down at his invasion, sucking him deeper, begging for more. Curling his fingers, he found the spot hidden deep inside and rubbed.

Above him, her whole body trembled.

She rode his hand, a confetti of condoms landing on the bed around them, across his chest. At least twenty of them.

"You plan to use all those tonight?"

"What?" she asked, her eyes glazed and unfocused. Her hips rolled with each push and pull of his fingers. Caught between them, his cock felt each slip and slide.

Enough, he wanted inside.

Changing gears to grasp her hips, Ty lifted her and set her farther back in his lap. Sweeping away the others on his chest, he grabbed a condom and rolled it on.

Van was waiting, eager, already up on her knees, poised to take him deep.

The expression of ecstasy that crossed her face…the way her eyes slid shut, drove straight to the center of him. Knowing he was the source of it did something to him.

It made him want to do this over and over again just so that he could see that moment. Made him want to roar with accomplishment and satisfaction. Made him want to take out a billboard so the entire world would know just what they had when they were together.

Instead, he savored the moment.

Bracing her hands on his shoulders, Van began to swirl her hips. She didn't wait for him to take control. She took what she wanted.

And that was sexy as hell.

Up and down, she rode him, head thrown back. She felt so damn good. Unbelievable.

But he wanted more.

Wrapping his palms around her face, he dragged her head down and demanded, "Open your eyes, Van. Look at me."

She did, her glazed stare finding his. Her hair spilled across the backs of his hands, so soft, just like her skin.

In that moment, neither of them could hide. He saw everything she was feeling in her eyes, her expression. Yes, pleasure. Joy. But more. There was something bigger, building, growing. Fed by the connection and history that they shared. Nurtured by the understanding and recognition that they each saw the other for who they really were—not who they chose to show the rest of the world.

Ty could feel the explosion building at the base of his spine, but gritted his teeth and willfully held it back. He could feel Van's body winding tighter and tighter, her strokes becoming more and more erratic.

Grasping her hips, Ty helped her, guided her. His hips arched up off the bed, deepening each thrust so that they were as connected as humanly possible.

Her entire body quivered with it. "Ty. God. Oh."

"Let go, princess. Give it to me."

"I can't… I don't…"

"You can." His teeth ground together, fighting. "You will. Now."

Her body convulsed with the power of the orgasm that tore through her. But she kept her eyes trained on him. He saw the wonder, the bliss and the fear all swirling through her expression. She gave that to him, too.

But he barely had any time to dwell on that before the shuddering muscles of her sex pulled him over, too.

Ty groaned her name, throwing his head back and bucking into the beautiful delirium they'd found together.

His hands tightened on her. Part of him expected that she'd push him away again. That the fear he'd seen deep in her eyes would win.

But she surprised him—as she always did.

Instead, she collapsed onto the bed beside him, her legs tangled with his and an arm thrown across his chest.

Her deep, heavy breathing fluttered across his skin. After several minutes it slowed. He thought she'd fallen asleep, but when he moved to get up and dispose of the condom her leg and arm tightened, pinning him in place.

Rolling his head, Ty gazed down at her, getting only her profile and a single green eye that watched him.

"I need a minute. I'll be right back."

Her only answer was to ease up on her hold. Ty went to the bathroom, disposed of the condom and then returned, as promised. He paused beside the bed, waiting... for what?

Lifting an arm, she waited, too.

Something tightened in his chest, but Ty ignored it. Instead, he concentrated on the woman welcoming him back to bed.

Her legs tangled with his again and her arm snaked

over him. But this time, her fingers played softly over the ink on his skin.

"Don't hate me when I have to wake you up every two hours because of your concussion," she whispered.

"Princess, haven't you figured out that I could never hate you?"

12

THE CABIN WAS GORGEOUS, exactly what she'd had in mind when she'd dreamed about getting away from Texas. The air was softer, cooler than home. It didn't feel like she was trying to breathe in a solid brick of air.

They'd arrived about twenty minutes ago, unloading their luggage and getting Kaia settled in the cabin. But the mountains surrounding them had called her back outside.

Trees towered over her, over the house that was a hell of a lot larger than two people needed. In the distance she could see the jagged outline of the mountains. The sun was just starting to set, splashing soft color across the summer evening.

"It's beautiful," Van said, propping a hip against the porch railing and leaning her shoulders into the upright. "I could stay out here all night and just breathe it in."

Ty stepped up beside her, filling the space. He didn't actually touch her, but he didn't really have to. Her body reacted to his nearness anyway, coming alive.

"Who are you trying to kid? I give you thirty minutes before you're twitching like a junky going through withdrawal. You, Dr. Cantrell, are a workaholic and we both know it," he said, tweaking her nose.

Van batted his hand away. He wasn't wrong, although part of her wanted him to be.

She really had no idea how to just do nothing. "Fine. But I have a feeling if I could figure out how to settle anywhere, it would be somewhere like this. It has a… peace that I've never felt before."

Ty turned, his gaze peering out into the distance. They stood there in silence together for a little while, just soaking in the atmosphere. Eventually, they'd need to head back into town to grab some groceries, but for now the practical things could wait.

"You know, this place actually reminds me of Afghanistan."

Van's body stiffened. Tension pulled against every cell in her body. She forced herself to relax. To listen.

"What do you mean?"

"The mountains there are starker, not green like these, brown and harsh. But they're still beautiful, in their own way."

Hearing him say that surprised her. "Really?"

Ty threw her a quick, wry glance, as if he'd read her mind and understood exactly what she was thinking.

"We might be there to fight a war, but not everyone in the country is. There are men, women and children just trying to live their lives. The country can be harsh, but the people are so resilient."

The words he screamed when he woke up in her ER came rushing back to her. The people there weren't the only resilient ones…

"What happened over there?" she asked, her voice soft and careful.

She half expected him to brush her off. To give her

some half-assed answer. So she was shocked when he didn't.

Instead, he turned and leaned against the opposite post so he could look her square on. His expression was stark and more open than she'd seen...probably ever.

Even from the moment she met him as a little boy, Ty Colson had always seemed closed off. He kept secrets. She knew that. And it bothered her, both then and now.

Because even as a little girl, she'd understood the secrets he'd kept were bad. And she'd felt helpless because there wasn't anything she could do to help.

He'd hidden the truth from everyone, pretending things were okay. She knew what Ty looked like when he lied—cool, calm and in control.

And while he was all of those things, the haunted expression in his gaze told her that he wasn't hiding. Not now anyway.

"I already told you about the day he died."

Van shook her head. "No. I don't mean what happened to Ryan. What happened to you?"

His mouth pulled down at the edges, his words clipped and matter-of-fact. "I watched my best friend get blown up right in front of me."

Van swallowed, and debated leaving the topic alone. Did she really want to know? Did he really need her digging?

"Do you remember what you yelled when you woke up in the ER after your accident?"

"No." The single word was harsh and clipped.

"Well, it was clear that you'd been through something awful and were reliving those moments."

A harsh sound wheezed through his open lips.

Unable to stay away any longer, Van closed the space

between them. Her palms rested on his waist and she drew close, staring up at him.

He watched her, impassive. His hands hanging loose by his sides. They stood that way for several moments. He was still. Unnaturally still. His chest barely rose with each breath.

And then he was a blur of motion.

His arms tightened around her body, crushing her against him. His face buried in the crook of her neck, warm lips pressed tight to her skin.

She couldn't move. But in that moment, she didn't want to be anywhere else.

Van could feel his heartbeat speeding so fast. It thumped painfully against her, anxiety and adrenaline fueling his body's responses.

"Tell me," she whispered.

IF ONLY IT were that easy.

He'd been to therapy, a couple of times actually. And it helped. But not nearly as much as holding Savannah Cantrell in his arms.

When she was there, he finally felt whole.

"There's nothing to tell."

"We both know that's a lie, Ty."

He sighed, because she was right.

Her hands rested on his chest. The scent of her surrounded him, the sweet, spicy character of it overpowering the clear mountain air and filling him up.

He wanted to grab her and crush his mouth to hers, to distract them both, but something in her expression stopped him.

This was real. Right now. This moment. She was asking for a piece of him, a truth that he hadn't shared with anyone else. Not even Ryan.

The question was, could he give it to her without utterly breaking himself?

And if he didn't, could there be any hope for something more between them? Did he want that?

Yes. That single word rang through his head, clear and precise.

He wanted Van in his life. Not as his best friend's little sister. Not as some holdover from a childhood that carried more pain than joy. But as the woman he shared everything with.

But that actually meant he had to share everything.

"When you woke up in the ER, you started fighting against the straps holding you down. Screaming about letting you go. Not hurting you."

Ty sucked in a harsh breath. It was one thing to decide to open up to her. It was another to actually do it.

He'd locked the memories from that day away so long ago. Kept them hidden deep, because what good would it do to bring them out? No one cared. Not really.

No, that was the little boy inside him, bitter and wounded, coming out. Not the strong, capable man he'd become. The soldier skilled at combat and able to take down anyone who threatened the weak—himself included. He refused to let someone else's actions, however painful and destructive, color the person he was now.

There were people who cared. Even in his worst moments, Ryan, Van, Nick and Margaret had been there for him. Treating him like he belonged. Their love couldn't erase the fact that his own mother didn't give enough of a shit to protect him, but it didn't need to. Because they cared.

Those memories. Those examples were what had shaped him into the person he was. He'd fought against the fear, the inclination to simply roll himself into a protective little shell and keep everyone away. He wouldn't let that fear win now.

Not when the potential prize was something beautiful with Van.

Ty clenched his eyes shut and fought, with himself, with the past. He didn't open them before the words began to spill out.

"That night I ended up in the hospital when I was thirteen…"

He could feel her. The way she leaned into him, her body pressed tight against his. The flutter of her pulse beneath his fingers. He didn't remember reaching out for her and clasping his fingers along the curve of her throat.

"It was bad."

"No shit," she whispered. "I was there, Ty. I saw the damage. Everyone knows you didn't get those injuries doing some stupid stunt on your bike. For one thing, if that had happened we all know Ryan would have been right beside you in the next hospital bed over."

A wheeze of laughter broke through the haze of tension wrapped around him. He buried his face into the soft cloud of her hair. "God, I needed that laugh. You always know just what to do or say to shake me out of whatever shit is trying to grab hold."

Van wrapped her arms around his waist and squeezed. "You keep saying things like that and I'm liable to fall in love with you, soldier." Her tone and laughter made the words into a joke. But there was an edge of reality that Ty clung to. Because that's exactly what he wanted.

Rather than spook her by saying that, he carried on with the truth.

"You're right, though. Ryan called me on the shit story a few hours after I told it, and he only waited that long because he wanted to confront me when we were alone. I stuck to what I'd said. Told him I'd needed to get out of the house for a little bit and clear my head so I took the bike out by myself. He didn't believe me, but he didn't press."

Van's forehead, buried in his sternum, rolled back and forth. "He knew you needed the lie."

"Yeah."

A lump formed deep in Ty's throat. Shit. He missed his friend. Life was not the same without him and never would be again.

Clearing the emotion away, Ty said, "I can't even remember what started it. Probably because whatever it was wouldn't have mattered to anyone else. But to the asshole my mom was sleeping with, the infraction was worth a nightmare. I didn't even see the first blow coming."

Van's fingers clenched, digging painfully into his back. He didn't tell her or move her. He let the slight sting keep him grounded so that the memories wouldn't completely engulf him.

"I ended up sprawled on the floor. My mom just cackled. She stood behind him, her eyes bright, and watched as the bastard sent his steel-toed boot into my side five or six times."

"The broken ribs."

"Yep. But somehow I managed to get up, away. God, it hurt so damn bad, Van. The pain was just a fire spreading through my whole body. I'd never felt anything like that—not before or since. I've been in hand-to-hand combat, gotten injuries, been thrown to the ground by explosions. Nothing hurt like that."

"Of course not. You're a man, Ty. A rather large, muscular, well-trained one at that. You were prepared for those events when they happened to you. But back then, you were a thirteen-year-old boy exposed to people who were supposed to be protecting you, not hurting you."

Ty rolled his cheek, resting it on the crown of her head so he could stare out at the mountains spread before them. "Maybe, but I knew better. It wasn't like I ever had the safety and comfort that you and Ryan had."

She made a sound, low and deep in her throat. At first he thought it was a whimper, until he pulled back so that he could look into her eyes and saw the fierce anger shining there.

His warrior. How many times had she taken up for him when they were younger? Stood beside him and Ryan as they'd confronted some bully on the playground or single-handedly gave some witch a verbal tongue lashing for spreading rumors about him?

She was gorgeous all the time, but never more so than when she was on a crusade.

"God, I want to drive back to Watershed, knock on her door and send my fist right into her face," she growled.

Ty chuckled. That was something he'd pay good money to see. "She isn't worth it. I came to that conclusion long before I moved out of her house."

"Maybe not, but you are."

Shit. Her words, said in that fierce, no-nonsense tone, had his knees buckling. If it wasn't for the post at his back he might have sunk straight to the floor. Nothing got to him that way. Nothing except for the fiery woman in front of him.

He had no idea what to say, so he just shook his head. "He caught me by the hair, yanked me back and pounded the shit out of me a little more. I'm not sure why he stopped. I'm not sure what I did. It's possible I cried and screamed and begged for it to end."

He could hear his own grim tone of voice. Could hear the echo of his cries for mercy and hated himself a little for them. Maybe if he'd stood strong and not shown any weakness then he could live with the experience. Knowing he hadn't let them break him.

But they had. He'd broken that night. Not just because they'd hurt him physically, but because they'd played with him. Letting him think they were going to let him escape before his mom would pop up in front of him, blocking the exit.

"At one point she wrapped her arms around me. Started whispering in my ear. Apologizing. Telling me she loved me. I relaxed, thought she was going to make him leave me alone. Instead, she pinned my arms to my side and let him ram his fist into my belly. Then her words changed. She started screaming at me about getting Protective Services involved. She promised if they ever showed up again she wouldn't just let her boyfriend beat on me, she'd let him kill me. And I believed her."

Van gasped. She'd come to the same conclusion he had... Nick and Margaret were the only ones who might have known what was happening at home and called Protective Services, prompting the visit his mother had somehow managed to pass...and then punish him for.

But he'd never blamed Nick and Margaret. Quite the opposite—the fact that they'd tried to protect him meant more than they'd ever know.

He didn't realize Van was crying until a warm, wet

drop landed on the back of his hand. He stared at it for several seconds, his brain slow to process what he was seeing. When he realized what it was, his gaze jerked up to her, expecting to find her clear green gaze full of pain and sadness.

Instead, the fire that had been there moments before was blazing even brighter, the tears slowly rolling down her face doing nothing to quench the fierce anger she felt on his behalf.

"Seriously, if I ever see that woman I'm going to hurt her."

"Good to know, princess. I'll make sure you stay far away from her. Because she isn't worth potential jail time. Your safety and happiness is a hundred times more important to me than she'll ever be."

Van stared at him for several seconds, her gaze narrow and full of fight. Finally, she gave him a jerky, reluctant nod. "Keep going."

So she knew there was more. Ty debated; maybe he'd given her enough.

As if sensing his hesitation, she reiterated, "Finish the story."

"Fine. They locked me in a closet and then had sex on the sofa. I could hear him, her, while I was sitting in the dark cradling my busted ribs and throbbing face. Sometime in the middle of the night, when the house was quiet, I managed to use a thin piece of cardboard I found on the floor to open the lock. I walked to the ER and asked them to call your parents. You know the rest."

Van closed her eyes. Her skin was flushed and for the first time he realized that her hands were trembling.

"Hey," he whispered, bracketing her face with his hands. "It's over. Has been for a very long time. I'm fine."

"You keep saying that, Ty, but I honestly don't know how that's true. I mean, I believe it is. You're one of the most loyal, honest, strong and dedicated men I've ever met. How is that possible after what you've lived through?"

Her head tipped backward, she stared up at him, a whole host of emotions swirling in her gaze. She thought all of those things about him? *He* thought all of those things about her.

"That night, and others like it, are part of what made me who I am, Van. And I don't think I'd change any of it. They brought me Ryan, the best friend a man could ever have. And your parents, who gave me a better example. A better family. They brought me you."

Ty stooped to brush his lips across Van's soft, sweet mouth. The kiss was gentle, with none of the repressed anger, frustration or overwhelming passion that tended to swirl between them. This moment was more. Deeper.

It wasn't just about something physical. It was about a connection. Understanding. Sharing.

And then it was more. The moment morphed into a combination of it all, the passion crackling between them building on the tender moment, electrifying it with need.

Picking her up, Ty didn't wait for her reaction or permission. He palmed her thigh and wrapped it tight around his waist. The bulge of his erection hit her straight where she needed it most, an explosion of desire rocketing through her.

They stumbled together into the cabin, slamming the door shut. Kaia lifted her head, but didn't bother moving from the spot she'd found on a rug before the stone fireplace.

He wasn't going to make it to the bedroom, not when the need to be inside her was overwhelming.

13

WAKING UP BESIDE Ty was…amazing. Van's cheek rested against his hard shoulder. The warmth of his body and the drape of his arm across her waist made her feel protected and safe.

Something she hadn't realized she needed until she had it.

The problem was, she couldn't keep it. And she would have to remember that. No matter how perfect these moments might feel, they were fleeting. Nothing about what was happening between her and Ty was permanent.

So she couldn't let herself get too used to him being there.

With those unpleasant thoughts spinning through her head, Van gingerly picked up Ty's arm, shifted it off her body and rolled away.

She was almost at the edge of the bed when a hard band snaked around her waist and snatched her right back.

"Where do you think you're going?" he grumbled, his face buried into the crook of her neck.

"To shower."

"Why?"

"Because it's morning and that's what I always do when I wake up."

"Not today."

Van wasn't sure whether to be irritated or amused. "Oh, yeah?"

His body shifted, dragging her along until she was draped over him. He was naked, the thin sheet the only barrier between them, and it was definitely not enough to hide his morning wood.

"Shower later. Sleep now."

"I'm done sleeping." Van rolled her hips, satisfied at the deep groan she dragged from Ty. "Time to get up."

"When's the last time you spent an entire day in bed, doc?"

Van opened her mouth and then had to shut it again. She honestly couldn't remember. "High school. Maybe."

Ty pulled away, gazing up at her with sleepy eyes. "That's just sad."

"I don't like to be lazy."

"I have no intention of being lazy, princess." The knowing grin that melted across his face sent a warm burst of need tumbling through her veins. "I fully intend to work off plenty of calories with you, in between naps, snacks and binge-watching mindless television."

Van huffed. That sounded like the best and worst day ever. The sex she wanted. Like right now. The rest of it... "This could be a disaster, Ty."

"Trust me."

"Don't say I didn't warn you."

"The alternative is to call up a guy I know and schedule a rock-climbing excursion."

Shifting backward, Van ran her gaze across Ty's face, paying special attention to his eyes.

The first night after his accident, she'd woken him up every couple hours. Neither of them had been thrilled about that, but it was necessary. Yesterday, she'd refused to let him drive, which pissed him off. Too bad.

But so far he hadn't exhibited any signs of complications from his concussion.

"Any headache this morning?"

"No, but there is another part of me that hurts."

"What? Where?" In doctor mode, Van completely missed the twitch of his lips as she pushed at Ty's hands resting on her waist. Trying to scramble off him, she wanted a better look. Maybe she'd missed something on the X-rays. It would be like Ty not to mention that he was in pain. Idiotic man.

"Is it from the accident or something else? Your scans didn't show any internal injuries, but it's possible we missed something."

Van set her hands on his shoulders and started running them over his chest and belly, searching for signs of bruising beneath the colorful ink across his skin.

Her first indication that he was messing with her was the barely contained laughter in his voice. "A little lower, doc."

Van's eyebrows beetled. Her gaze moved to meet his, those gray-blue eyes filled with humor.

"Come on, princess. I ache," he said, pushing his hips up so that the erection straining against the sheet was impossible to miss.

"Asshole," she grumbled, smacking his shoulder. Flopping down onto the bed, Van settled onto her back... away from him.

"Aw, don't be like that." Ty rolled to his side, resting on a single elbow while he loomed over her. "I've never had a chance to play doctor with a real doctor before. Help me live out a teenage fantasy."

The imploring, little-boy expression on his face was wholly fake and absolutely endearing. Van tried to stay stern and firm, but she couldn't pull it off.

"God, you're incorrigible, you know that?"

"You say that like it's a bad thing."

On anyone else, she'd think it was. But on Ty...it simply reminded her just how much he hadn't been able to act like this when he was really a child. Who was she to deny him the opportunity to be silly now that he had the chance?

"Fine. Whatever. We'll spend the day in bed."

The smile he gifted her with was enough reward, although the orgasms he clearly had in mind wouldn't go unappreciated.

"Rock climbing tomorrow."

"A nice, easy hike in the mountains tomorrow. Maybe rock climbing the next day. Doctor's orders."

"Fine. Whatever," he said, throwing her own words back at her.

He didn't wait for her reaction, just took advantage of his position. Grasping her waist, he pulled her beneath him, pressing his mouth against her naked skin.

Whatever he wanted, he could have. That was the problem with Ty Colson. He knew exactly how to maneuver her...and make her like it.

"ROMANTIC COMEDY."

"Spaghetti Western." Ty watched Van for any sign of weakness. Any break in her expression to tell him he'd hit on a genre that gave him an advantage. Nope, not spaghetti Westerns.

She countered with "Historical drama."

"God, kill me now. B-grade horror."

Ah, there it was. A tiny flicker of interest in the back of her gaze. One she tried to bank, but one he saw anyway.

They'd spent most of the morning in bed, dozing off and on between bouts of amazing sex. At some point he'd gotten up, checked on Kaia and made sure she had plenty of food and water before bringing back sandwiches he'd thrown together.

"Every episode of *Say Yes to the Dress*."

He groaned. "Are you trying to drive me back to the ER from self-inflicted wounds? No self-respecting man would agree to an entire day of watching a sappy show about women trying on wedding dresses."

Van's eyebrow quirked up. "Exactly how do you know what S*ay Yes to the Dress* is about?"

"I plead the fifth. And my final offer is a marathon of B-grade horror films."

He had her. He knew it when she gave a huge, overly dramatic sigh. "All right, but you owe me."

"Uh-huh." Ty browsed through his Netflix account until he found the perfect movie starring some big-chested, too-stupid-to-live scream queen. "The special effects in this one are going to be great."

"Don't you mean awful?"

"Yeah, that's what I said. The worse the effects, the better the experience."

Van rolled her eyes and let her body slip down the headboard of the bed. "You're mental."

Ty bounded back onto the bed, wrapped an arm around her waist and pulled her into his body. "Not according to my doctor."

Van reached over and pinched him in the side. Ty jumped. "Ow, what was that for?"

"Taking the name of your doctor in vain."

"Bloodthirsty little thing."

"You're the one making me watch hours of blood and guts."

Ty found the perfect spot right beneath her ribs and dug his fingers in.

Van screamed, jerked away from him and let out a loud peal of laughter.

"Now who's the one screaming? You know you're going to enjoy the melodramatic acting and oozing blood. Admit it. You have a bit of a sadistic streak you keep well hidden."

"No," she wheezed, struggling to get away from his tickling fingers. "I'll never admit to anything."

This called for a double assault.

Ty brought his mouth down onto her parted lips and swept his tongue inside. The heat was immediate and overwhelming. It always was whenever he touched her. The need for her was never ending. Just when he thought he had it banked, she'd do or say something that would send the urge to touch her, taste her, consume her, spiking through him.

"Admit it," he murmured against her lips. "I promise your secret will be safe with me."

"Fine," she huffed out. "I'm a closet horror fan. There, are you happy?"

Ty pulled away, a grin twisting his lips. Laughter and joy bubbled up inside his chest. He couldn't remember the last time he'd ever felt like this…carefree.

Van stared up at him, her eyes wide and swimming with unshed tears of laughter.

God, he wanted this moment to last forever.

Suddenly, the atmosphere around them shifted. Or maybe it was something deep inside him.

He wanted her forever. The realization didn't stun him, not like it should have. It was more like a quiet understanding and acceptance.

Of course he wanted her forever. Savannah Cantrell was an amazing woman—loving, dedicated, brilliant and a marshmallow beneath that strong exterior she liked to show the world.

The laughter slowly slipped from her gaze. Ty let his fingers play across her jawline.

"Yes, I am happy. Probably more happy in this moment than I've ever been in my entire life."

She swallowed, the long column of her elegant throat drawing his attention.

"Ty, you can't say things like that," she whispered.

"Why not?"

"Because you're leaving in a few days. And that's not what this is."

Placing her hands on his shoulders, Van pushed him away.

Ty rocked backward, letting his body hit the headboard with a loud thud.

Her words hurt. More than he wanted to admit.

He was used to rejection. Used to being unwanted.

Ty thought he'd become so numb to that experience that nothing would ever be able to touch him that way again.

Apparently, he was wrong.

But he refused to let Van see that she'd wounded him. Number one lesson that he'd learned early in life: showing weakness only revealed something to be exploited and used against you.

Dragging a steady voice from somewhere deep, Ty said, "Yeah, you're right. That's not what this is."

Grabbing the remote, he turned up the volume, wrapped an arm around her waist and pulled her against his side. Pillows piled behind them, covers tangled around them, they snuggled down to watch the movie.

The scream queen popped on screen in her tight pink sweater and flowing blond ringlets and within three minutes was running for her life covered in really bad fake blood. Over the next several hours they shared popcorn and picked apart non-existent plot lines in that movie and then two more.

But Ty's heart was no longer in it the way it had been.

THE DAY HAD started out so well. And had ended fine. After those few moments of tension between them, they'd found their way back to a comfortable camaraderie—mostly thanks to bad acting and terrible special effects.

They'd laughed, joked and eaten junk food. At one point, Kaia joined them, taking up more than half the bed.

Her presence was a buffer, one they'd both needed.

But there was something missing. And despite knowing it wasn't a good idea, Van wanted it back. She wanted the easy bond they'd developed over the last few days.

In an attempt to find it again, the next morning, over eggs, bacon, pancakes and fried potatoes, Van suggested they take Kaia out for a hike.

Ty's gaze narrowed. "You're letting me out of the house?"

"We're going on a hike, not climbing Mt. Everest. I don't even plan to break a sweat."

Snagging her around the waist, Ty lifted her into the air and plopped her back down into his lap. His mouth found the curve of her neck, sucking and licking his way up to the spot right behind her ear that always made her shiver. "I can think of better ways to work up a sweat anyway."

She was tempted to let him have his way. It would be so easy to give in to the desire that was spreading through her. But she needed some distance—a break—if she had any hope of keeping her heart intact when it was time for him to leave.

So, pushing away from him, she rose to her feet. "Hike now. Sex later."

With a huff, Ty glared up at her. "Spoilsport."

She shrugged. "My dog needs exercise."

The words fell off her tongue easily. More easily than she'd have expected only weeks ago. Somehow, over the last few days, Kaia had become her dog. Not Ryan's. Not the military's. She was Van's, worming her way straight into her heart.

At least, when everything was said and done, she'd have Kaia in her life. No longer alone.

The thought was cold comfort when Ty wrapped his arm around her waist and dragged her down the hallway toward the bedroom.

"Fine. Hurry up, then. The sooner we get on with it, the sooner we'll be home, the sooner I can get you naked again."

Ty pushed her into the bedroom ahead of him, swatting her rear. Van squealed, growled and tossed a glare over her shoulder. "You'll pay for that later."

"Lord, I hope so."

Van threw on some cargo shorts, a lightweight T-shirt,

thick socks and the hiking boots she'd pulled out of the closet back home. Snatching a ball cap Ty had left sitting on the dresser, she pulled her long hair through the hole in the back, letting the loose tail trail behind her.

"Hey, that's mine."

Tossing him a saucy grin, Van said, "Not anymore," and dashed out of the room, leaving him tugging a dark gray shirt over his head.

She didn't bother with makeup, just some moisturizer with sunscreen. It was nice knowing Ty didn't give a rip if she put on concealer, mascara and lipstick. With him, she could just be herself.

Grabbing a few supplies for Kaia, she stuffed them into a small pack and started to fling it over her shoulder. The bag was caught midarc and snagged out of her hand. "What kind of man would I be if I let you carry that?"

"The kind that recognizes I'm perfectly capable of carrying my own bag."

"Of course you are, but that doesn't mean you should have to."

A bright sensation bubbled up inside her chest. Ty gave a shrill whistle. Kaia jumped up and loped over to them. "I'm not sure how much of a hike she'll be up for." A frown tugged at the corners of Ty's mouth.

Van hadn't even thought about that. Kaia approached her disability with such calm and acceptance that Van often forgot she didn't have a leg. It didn't seem to slow her down, not one bit.

But then, they hadn't set out for a hike in the Rocky Mountains before.

"Maybe we shouldn't go."

"Nope. We'll take our cues from her and see. Gotta

try it sometime. Besides, she loves to hike. It's kinda part of the job description…long marches."

Van sucked in a deep breath and held it. Ty talked about his life in Afghanistan so flippantly. Like it just was. And she supposed that was true. For him, marching for miles in the rough countryside loaded down with supplies and gear was business as usual.

The same had been true for Kaia.

Staring at him, she wondered if Ty would handle the transition back to civilian life as well as Kaia had.

And when that might be.

He wasn't as young as he used to be. The wear and tear on his body had to be making itself known. In fact, she'd noticed him rubbing at his knee after that long run when Kaia bolted at the parade.

How long until he gave up the life? Had he even started thinking about it?

God, she wanted to ask him. Hope bloomed inside her chest. But she was afraid to. Afraid of an answer she didn't want to hear.

The military was all Ty had ever known. Would anything be able to convince him to leave that work behind? Leave the dogs?

Van didn't want to ask the question only to find out the answer was that his career, the dogs, meant more than she ever could. That would hurt worse than him simply leaving.

They piled into the car and headed for the mountains. Ty seemed to know exactly where they were going so Van didn't ask. Instead, she stared out the window, her mind racing and her spirit plummeting with each unhappy thought.

After about twenty minutes they pulled into a little

parking area at the head of a trail. Several vehicles occupied the lot, but there were no people. They were probably all out on the trails.

Ty let Kaia out of the car. Van moved a little slower. She'd just closed her door when a warm wall of male pressed up against her back. Hands on her waist, Ty turned her and flattened her against the curved body of the vehicle.

"Whatever's going on in that pretty head of yours, stop it."

Van's startled gaze met his, then darted away as his words sank in.

"I'm not sure what you mean."

Hands bracketing her face, Ty forced her to meet his stare.

"Oh, I think you do, princess. I can see the frown lines crinkling your brows." The soft pad of his index finger trailed over the offending spot.

Van batted his hand away. "Gee, thanks for pointing out that I'm developing lines on my face. What every girl dreams of hearing."

"Van."

"What?"

"Shut up," he said, right before his lips brushed softly against her own.

She couldn't help it. She responded, melting against him and grabbing hold. Her fingers curled into his biceps.

After several seconds he pulled away. She was left breathless. His blue eyes, so deep and close, stared down at her.

"Whatever's got your head spinning, leave it alone for a little while."

Nodding, Van's tongue slipped out to trail moisture across her suddenly dry lips.

The three of them set off on the path, the world around them gorgeous. Lush and green. Harsh rocks jutting out from fresh growth and bright colors of summer. The blue sky hung overhead, unbroken and cloudless.

"I read there's a waterfall ahead."

"You read?"

"Yep. The internet is a wonderful thing. Interested in seeing it?"

"Absolutely."

Kaia ran ahead of them, bounding off her leash with exuberant joy. Every few paces she'd glance back at Ty, though, checking in to see if he needed her. She sniffed at trees, nosed at rocks and darted several feet into the underbrush.

The first time she did it, Van startled, pulling at Ty's hand wrapped around hers so she could dart after the dog.

But he wouldn't let her go.

"She's fine."

The anxiety in her chest wasn't certain it agreed with Ty, but looking into his calm, steady gaze, she gave him a reluctant nod.

They walked in companionable silence. But the sounds of nature surrounded them—birds, small rodents, leaves rustling. The air was clear and crisp, the heat of the day not yet baking everything in sight.

Between them, Ty swung their hands in a gentle motion that felt natural…right.

And slowly, Van felt the tension that always held her body in its tight grip slipping away.

"This is nice."

"Mmm," Ty agreed.

About an hour in, she started hearing gentle sounds of water rushing over rocks. Around a bend in the trail they joined with a small stream. Water frothed over rocks and flowed easily into the darker line of forest around them.

They continued until the gentle babble began to pick up speed and became a dull roar. Then grew louder and louder.

Breaking through the line of trees, Van sucked in a sharp breath. "It's beautiful."

The falls weren't big, but they weren't exactly small, either. Water, probably fed from the melting snowcaps at the top of the peaks in the distance, rushed over ragged rocks to drop into a churning pool in the stream they'd been following for the last fifteen minutes.

The power of it was awe-inspiring. "So amazing to see what Mother Nature can do. Impressive."

Ty didn't comment, just squeezed her hand and then led her around the curve of the pool to the far side, where he dropped the pack, zipped it open and pulled out one of those silver survival blankets. Spreading it on the ground, he dropped several containers she hadn't seen him pack.

"What's all this?"

Sending her a lopsided grin, he said, "I figured we'd need some fuel for the trek back."

First, he pulled out a bowl and filled it with water from a bottle. Setting it alongside another with dog food at the edge of the blanket, Ty raised his voice and issued a command for Kaia to come.

Seconds later, she bounded out of the woods.

Van could have sworn a smile stretched her doggy face as she skidded to a halt beside them. Dropping onto her haunches, tongue lolling out of her mouth, she regarded both of them before turning her attention to the bowls Ty had set out.

Kaia taken care of, Ty started preparing their own meal. It wasn't fancy—crackers, cheese, grapes, strawberries, beef jerky and some trail mix. Digging deep into the pack, he tossed Van a water bottle, keeping another for himself. For the next little while, they talked and laughed and ate. At some point Ty grabbed her by the waist and spun her around so that she was leaning against him, her head pillowed against his thigh.

His fingers ran through her hair in a soothing rhythm. With a loud sigh, Kaia plopped down onto her belly beside them. Sunshine splashed across her body, warming her and leaving her drowsy.

Drowsy, with a full belly and her body pleasantly fatigued from the hike, that was the last thing Van remembered.

14

Ty STARED DOWN at Van. She looked so different while sleeping. Her features were less taut and focused. She looked more like the girl he remembered than the woman she'd become. Not that he didn't appreciate the woman she'd grown into.

But he knew Van and understood just how much pressure and expectation she placed on her own shoulders.

It was nice to see some of that tension disappear.

Especially when she was cuddled up in his lap.

Back pressed against the trunk of a tree, Ty let his own body relax.

They were alone out here, at least for the moment. His fingers were tangled in her hair, the silky strands caressing the back of his hand. His other rested on her hip.

Her head was turned, her face nearly even with the dull throb of his half erection.

It would be easy to wake her up and take advantage of the moment. To turn it hot and passion filled. And maybe he'd do that later.

But for right now, this moment was more than sex. It was more than their shared history. It was comfort and an easiness he'd never found with anyone else. Sitting here, watching her sleep was more fulfilling than any sexual encounter he'd had with another woman.

That serenity pulled at him, tempting him to join her for a little nap. The last few days had taken a toll on him, more than he'd expected. He'd been injured before and hadn't taken the time to let those wounds stop him.

But the accident and this concussion seemed to affect him more than anticipated.

Or maybe he was just getting old.

Either way, Ty gave in to the urge.

And woke up to a nightmare.

A loud, frantic bark from Kaia followed by an ungodly roar jolted Ty awake. He'd been in enough war zones that he could be sound asleep one second and standing on his feet with a gun in his hand sighting onto an enemy in the next.

Today, it took him longer to come to, mostly because he couldn't simply vault to his feet. Not with Van stretched out and cuddled up in his lap.

But his brain was immediately awake and taking in the scene in front of him.

"Oh, shit," he breathed, picking Van up with him and setting her onto her feet.

"What?" she muttered sleepily.

"Wake up. Now," Ty growled, urgency making his words rough.

Another loud roar ripped through their little clearing followed by a rolling warning from Kaia.

That jolted Van. He felt it, the moment she came awake and realized what was happening.

On the edge of the clearing, just on the other side of the stream, a black bear stood on its hind legs, mouth open. Its razor-sharp teeth gleamed in the sunshine as spit flew from its mouth in a god-awful bellow of warning.

One that Kaia was ignoring.

Back bristling, hair standing on end, the dog stood with her legs spread wide and her own teeth bared. Her body quivered, every muscle ready to spring and strike.

She'd been trained for attack, to bring down foes on command. But not even a three-hundred-pound man could match the damage a black bear could do.

"Kaia, no," Ty yelled.

The black bear's head swiveled, its beady eyes wide with outrage. Cold fear washed over Ty's body. His palms itched for a weapon that wasn't there. Stupid.

Beside him, Van shifted. The bear took a lumbering step forward, setting a single paw into the cool, lapping water.

"Don't move."

Shit. He wasn't going to be able to protect her. Either of them. Not if that bear decided to charge across the stream.

Frustration, helplessness and grief welled up inside him. This was Ryan all over again. He'd stood by and watched as his friend had been killed, unable to do anything. The only difference in that situation and this one was that now he could see the disaster coming.

But still, he couldn't do anything to stop it.

His heart thudded erratically in his chest. Adrenaline flooded his system, useless since he couldn't do a damn thing with it.

Kaia, countering the movement of the bear, charged a foot into the stream herself. The bear's attention swung back to her, but that was cold comfort.

Neither he nor Van would sit by and watch the bear attack Kaia. He wouldn't be able to do nothing, and he knew Van well enough to realize her savior complex wouldn't allow her to, either.

"Kaia, stop." Ty issued the command with a strong, stern tone, hoping her training would trump the survival instincts pushing her right now.

The dog swung her head so that she could see Ty from the corner of her eye. He issued the command again. "Kaia, stop."

She whimpered, her body language changing. That was a good sign. He wanted her away from the edge of the stream, but the bear was close enough that if she moved suddenly it might trigger an attack.

"Slowly, girl. Come."

The bear swung its head back and forth and let out another loud growl. Kaia's body quivered, but she didn't answer. Instead, she backed out of the stream onto the bank.

"Van, slowly, reach down and grab the bag. Leave everything else."

None of the things he'd taken out of the pack were important enough to risk their lives over. Nothing mattered except getting Van and Kaia out of there in one piece.

Hope spun inside his chest, fragile and warm.

Grasping her hand, Ty slowly edged them both sideways, away from the bear and toward Kaia. The forest might offer them some cover and distance.

Crouched low, Kaia crawled backward toward them. The bear shifted on its massive legs, its entire body shaking as it issued one more roar in their direction. But it was no longer standing or poised to attack.

Kaia paused, her gaze swinging between the bear and Ty, as if struggling over whether to face the threat or listen to her handler.

"It's fine, girl. We're gonna leave her alone and she'll leave us alone. Don't do anything rash."

Her ears pricked, and after several tense seconds, she began to ease backward again. The three met up at the edge of the woods. Ty reached down and grasped the harness strapped across Kaia's chest.

It wasn't often he felt the need to hold onto her; she was so good at following commands. But right now, he needed the reassurance of that strap against his palm.

Van walked behind him. He could feel the tension rolling off her. The harsh in and out of her breath as she fought the same panic trying to rush through his system.

"Don't turn around until you can't see it anymore," he cautioned.

Just as they edged behind some trees a couple feet into the forest Ty watched two cubs lumber out from behind some rocks and crash into their mother. She gave a rebuking sound and swatted gently at them. Her gaze stayed trained on the spot where they'd slipped into the forest.

"Oh, my God," Van breathed. Her hand gripped his shoulder. "She was protecting her babies."

Crap. "There's nothing worse than a mother bear defending her young."

They'd gotten seriously lucky.

The two cubs, probably six or seven months old, tumbled into the stream. They splashed together, rolling around in the shallows and making little bleating noises.

"They're kinda cute," Van sighed.

"Those cute bears nearly cost us our lives."

Ty had no idea what he would do if something happened to Van. He couldn't take it, not losing her, too.

But, wasn't that inevitable?

Hadn't she pretty much told him this was simply a fling? A circumstance of convenience?

She didn't see a future for them long-term.

How could she?

Savannah Cantrell was perfect. What did he really have to offer her except a high school education, fifteen years of military experience, and a shit-ton of bad memories that haunted him on a regular basis.

They only had a couple more days before this stolen trip to paradise came to an end and he found himself back in a war zone again.

Never before had the thought of returning to work left him feeling unhappy and anxious.

He loved his job. He loved the guys he worked with. He loved knowing that what he did saved lives and made a difference in the world.

Today, the thought of going back made him want to roar, just like the bear they'd left behind.

THE INCIDENT WITH the bear had scared the crap out of her. An hour later, her hands were still trembling, her body crashing from the flood of adrenaline. Her muscles ached. Between the hike out and the drive home, it felt like forever before they walked in the front door.

"I don't think I'll ever go hiking again." Van collapsed onto the sofa. Kaia curled up in what was becoming her spot in front of the fireplace, letting out a huge harrumphing sigh of agreement.

Van didn't even have a chance to get comfortable before her stomach growled, alerting her to the fact she hadn't eaten much. "Give me a minute and I'll fix us something to eat."

They'd left the food and blanket in the middle of the

forest. Now that they were away from the situation, she regretted having to leave their things for someone else to find and clean up. However, under the circumstances they'd really had no other choice.

Some critter—probably momma with her baby bears—was going to get a nice snack out of the food they'd left.

"Don't worry about it," Ty said, dropping onto the couch beside her. His arm went around her shoulders, pulling her into his body.

It was nice. Comforting. Safe.

Honestly, the entire situation could have been so much worse. But the thing she'd realized in the middle of it was that she wasn't nearly as concerned as she probably should have been. Because she knew Ty would do anything to make sure she and Kaia weren't harmed.

That's the kind of man he was.

Not that she wanted him to risk his own life to protect hers…that's what he did whether she liked it or not.

Shit. She was in deep.

In a little over a week Ty had somehow managed to become an integral part of her life. Something that became more obvious as they worked together to fix dinner, moving effortlessly in the kitchen. Sharing space without discussion. Compensating and accommodating automatically.

Standing at the stove, Ty stirred the chicken in a sauté pan, laughing at something she'd said. Struck by how handsome and domestic he looked, Van simply stared, taking in the expression on his face. Lightness and joy. The tiny crinkles at the edges of his eyes and lips. The sparkle in his gray-blue gaze. The deep, rolling, effervescent timbre of his laughter.

The moment, carefree and unimportant on the surface, lanced through her like the sharpened edge of a scalpel.

She loved him.

No, she was in love with this man.

Because she'd loved him for years. How could she not? Even when she was angry with him and blamed him for Ryan's choices, she'd cared about him.

But this was different. This was more.

Somewhere in the last few days she'd fallen for the man he'd become. Hard. And the thought of him not being in her life hurt.

A lot.

But there was nothing she could do to change the inevitable. Van had plenty of experience accepting difficult realities. She'd had to call *time of death* more often than she'd ever want to. And that moment of acknowledging the inevitable was always difficult. Saying goodbye hurt.

In a few days she'd have to do it again. Only this time, that moment would be personal in a way Van wasn't prepared for.

At least she could put it off a little while longer.

Shaking off the melancholy, Van pasted a smile onto her face and joined Ty at the stove. She wrapped her arm around his waist, pressed up onto her tiptoes and claimed his mouth with hers.

The kiss was quick and deep. She needed the taste of him on her tongue. Needed the warmth of him beneath her hands.

She pulled back. Ty stared down at her, his body suddenly still. "What was that for?"

"For protecting us today."

"I didn't do anything."

"You kept control of the situation. Your calm kept

me from panicking. And we both know if that bear had charged, you would have shielded me and Kaia without a second thought. That's the kind of man you are, Ty. And while I would have been seriously pissed had you gotten yourself hurt or killed because of your hero complex, I appreciate your integrity. That quality is rare in most of the men I see these days."

Ty gave her a cocky, lopsided grin. "Princess, you're hanging around the wrong men."

Bopping her fingertip onto his nose, Van said, "Apparently," and shifted to move away.

The insistent band of his arm kept her in place. "I'd do anything to keep you from pain, Van."

"I know," she whispered, pressing her lips against the curve of his neck. She breathed him in, his strong, male scent filling her lungs and making her crave more.

Something wet pressed against Van's hand resting on Ty's hip. She glanced down at Kaia, sitting on her haunches and staring up at them both, an expectant expression on her face.

"I think your dog wants her dinner," Ty laughed, the sound lightening the mood.

Van grabbed some of the cooked chicken from Ty's pan and plopped it into Kaia's bowl. She deserved a reward after her harebrained attempt at protecting them from a bear.

They didn't bother sitting at the large table in the open dining room beside the kitchen. That felt too formal for the night. She wanted to be snuggled up beside him.

So they took their plates to the den and held them on their laps. Occasionally, Ty would offer her his fork and she'd open her mouth to take the bite, delighting in the way his sharp gaze watched her lips and tongue.

They turned on some show on the Science channel about a team of ex-navy SEALs salvaging a Civil War ship. It was fascinating, but not nearly as captivating as watching Ty.

Eventually, he took her empty plate from her, ran the water and dropped everything in a sink full of suds.

She expected him to grasp her hand and lead her to bed. Instead, he settled back onto the sofa, stretching out and draping her across his prone body.

Van could feel the beat of his heart beneath her hands piled over his chest. His warmth settled deep inside her. His hard, muscled body should have been an uncomfortable mattress, but he wasn't.

How could it be with his hands slowly drifting up and down her body? His fingers worked their way beneath the hem of her shirt and the waistband of her jeans, over and over again brushing her skin softly. Crackles of electricity chased his movements, building and building until Van thought she might go mad if he didn't do something more. It was slow, delightful, agonizingly sweet torture.

When she'd finally had enough, Van reached down and tugged her shirt over her head. She flicked the clasp of her bra open, discarding that as well.

"What are you doing?" he asked, laughter tingeing his voice.

"Bastard," she breathed. "You know exactly what you've been doing to me for the last half hour." Rolling sideways, Van flicked the button open on her shorts and in one fluid motion pushed them and her panties down her legs. Kicking them, she sent them flying into the floor.

Reaching for his hand, Van guided him straight to where she needed him most. Propping one leg up, she pressed his fingertips against her moist sex and then slowly eased them inside.

Ty simply watched her, that swirling, stormy gaze devouring her. He made her feel like the center of his world, something that was entirely addictive.

Because she wasn't. Not really.

But for right now, she'd take the moment and cherish it.

Dropping to her knees, Van unbuttoned the fly on his jeans and tugged. Ty lifted his hips so she could pull them and his boxer shorts to the tops of his thighs.

God, he was gorgeous. All tanned skin and sinewy muscle. And the stark black ink that curled over the edge of his hip, following that tempting V that arrowed to his groin…yummy.

Leaning forward, Van ran her tongue across the lines, following the path straight to the erection straining upward.

He was long and hard. Soft skin over steel. And the minute she took him deep into her mouth she knew she'd never get enough of him. Of the salty, tangy taste of him. Of the low rumble of his growl. Or the way his fingers tangled in her hair, pulling her closer and silently begging her for more.

Van sucked, pulling him in until the head of his cock nudged the back of her throat. And still, she wanted more.

She pulled back, letting just the edge of her teeth scrape lightly over his skin. At the tip, she let her tongue play against the ridge of flesh, rubbing the sweet spot right beneath the head.

Over and over she sucked him deep and then played on her way back up. His fingers tightened until he was tugging gently at her hair. And even that felt good, evidence that she could drive him as completely mental with wanting as he'd done to her.

Van let her hands play across his chest, pushing his shirt out of the way so she could flick at the flat disc of his tightened nipple. Her other hand found the tight, heavy sack tucked between his legs and massaged.

He panted, hot and hard. She wanted to feel him in her mouth again. Feel him explode with pleasure.

But Ty wasn't content with that.

His big hands grasped her hips, pulling her up onto his lap. From somewhere, a condom appeared between his fingers and Van snatched it away so she could open and roll it over his erection.

Sheathed, Ty rolled them until her back was pressed to the sofa. Hooking one of her legs over the back of it, he spread her wide and pushed deep inside.

His eyelids flickered, as if they wanted to close, but he refused to let them. Instead, he stared at her, his gaze deep and open. Something sharp and heavy settled inside her chest. Love, happiness and the pain she knew was inevitable.

But not even that was enough to ruin this moment.

"God, Van. You feel so good. I just want to stay like this, locked together. To keep the entire world out." He flexed his hips, but otherwise stayed perfectly still.

Van could feel the width and breadth of him, buried deep inside her. Her body throbbed for him to move, to put an end to the ache swelling inside her.

But the rest of her agreed with him. As long as they stayed like this, poised on the edge, it felt like nothing could come between them.

"I keep thinking about this afternoon. Replaying those moments and coming up with a different outcome. What if Kaia hadn't listened? What if the bear had charged anyway? I was helpless, Van, without my gun. I couldn't have done anything to save her. Save you."

A shudder went through his body. Connected as they were, Van felt it.

She wrapped her arms around him and pulled him flush against her. His forehead landed in the crook of her throat, the warmth of his breath sweeping over her.

"But you did save us, with nothing but your instinct and training. Kaia and I are fine. Stop worrying about what might have happened and love me, Ty. Please."

Van flexed her hips, driving them up and pulling him deeper.

He groaned and then gave her exactly what she wanted. Grasping her hands, Ty twined their fingers together. He stroked deep and then pulled back, over and over, each thrust tinged with desperation and purpose. Ty needed this. *She* needed this.

Lost in the sensations he was creating, Van gave herself up to their joining. Ty knew exactly how to touch her and within minutes the orgasm was rolling through her, bigger, better and more overwhelming than ever before.

Ty joined her, not with a roar of her name that the world might hear, but a whisper just for her. "Only you, Van. Always you."

15

THE BUZZ OF the phone woke him. Ghostly light flickered across his eyes and it took him a moment to realize it came from the TV.

Exhausted from the adventures of the day, they'd fallen asleep. He'd probably pay for that mistake with a stiff neck and a sore back, but at the moment he didn't give a shit.

Van's naked body was stretched out over his, her warm, fragrant skin tempting him to wake her up for round two before tucking them both into bed.

Her soft brown hair was spread out across his chest. Somehow, his fingers had gotten tangled in the strands, his palm cupping the curve of her neck.

Ty shifted, about to lean down and run his lips over her shoulder when his phone buzzed again.

There were only a few people who had this number and no call this late could be good.

Cursing beneath his breath, Ty gently untangled his body, rolling Van so he disturbed her as little as possible, and then slipped out from under her.

Snatching up his cell, Ty saw he had two missed calls from his commander.

Shit. This was not going to be good at all.

He punched a button to return the call, the feeling of being screwed only reinforced by his CO answering after the first ring.

"Colson."

"Sir?"

"I hate to disturb you so late, but you're needed back ASAP."

"I'm on leave for another three days, sir."

"Not anymore. You're needed for a time-sensitive, top-level mission."

Ty wanted to argue. He opened his mouth to, but knew he couldn't. His CO wouldn't call if it wasn't important. They'd worked together for years. The other man knew exactly what had brought him home…he'd worked with Ryan as well.

That didn't mean Ty had to like it.

"When?" he ground out.

"Now. I've got a transport on standby at Schriever, ready to take you as soon as you arrive."

"Do I want to know how you know I'm in Colorado?"

A low chuckle coasted down the line. "Probably not."

Running a hand through his hair in frustration, Ty said, "All of my gear is back in Watershed."

"Have someone ship it to you."

A foul curse slipped from between his lips. Ty's teeth ground together. Tension shot up his jaw, settling as a dull ache at his temples.

"You know I wouldn't ask this, Colson, if there was another choice. Trust me when I say we need you back here and we need you here now."

There was a time in his life when he would have thrived on this kind of shit. Eaten up the fact that he'd been called in because of his specialized skills and superior training, his body buzzing with the promise of adrenaline and excitement.

But that was before Ryan.

Before Van.

At the moment, all he felt was tired. Right down to his bones.

Pulling in a deep breath, Ty closed his eyes and gave the only answer he could. "I'll be there as soon as I can, but I have to make sure someone is taken care of first."

"Well, do it quickly. We have a crisis here and a small window of opportunity to fix it. Lives are hanging in the balance."

They always were. The pressure had never bothered him before. But it did today. Because a few months ago Ty wouldn't have questioned his ability to handle whatever mission was put in front of him. And come out successful and whole.

Ever since Ryan's death, he'd lost that cocky confidence, the razor's edge that made him sharp and kept him fearless.

Rubbing a hand over his face, Ty disconnected the call, knowing he wouldn't get any more information from his CO on an unsecured cell phone, and dropped it down to his side.

He stared out the window into the clear Colorado sky. The stars were gorgeous, plentiful and so huge they cast enough light he could see halfway across the yard.

He needed to pack his stuff. Wake Van. Make arrangements for her and Kaia to get on a flight back home. He didn't like the idea of her staying out here alone, especially after the incident with the bear.

But he didn't want to do any of those things.

The last week and a half hadn't been perfect. And yet, he still didn't want to let it go.

He didn't want to let her go.

A soft sound warned him that she was awake. But Ty didn't turn away from the window. Maybe if he stayed right here they could both pretend that the world outside had stopped, leaving them cocooned inside forever.

He felt her, the roar of energy that crackled across his skin any time she was near.

"You're leaving."

It wasn't a question. Maybe she'd heard his end of the conversation. Or maybe she was just damned smart and had jumped to the same conclusion he had when his phone had rung in the middle of the night.

Twisting his head, Ty took her in. She'd grabbed the quilt draped across the back of the sofa and wrapped it around her body. Ty really wished she hadn't done that. He wanted to see her one last time.

Moonlight washed across her dark hair, giving the soft, rumpled curls a silvery glow. Her green eyes shimmered, not with heat or happiness—like she deserved—but with anger. He couldn't exactly blame her.

He'd promised her a week away and was bailing on her.

"I'm needed for a mission."

A low growl rolled up through her chest. On the other side of the room, Kaia's ears pricked at the noise. It startled them both, that fierce expression of Van's unhappiness. Especially when her face was as passive and blank as a calm lake.

He reached for her. Van jerked back, making sure he was too far away to connect with her. "Don't."

At first, he thought she meant don't touch. Until she continued.

"Don't go, Ty. Please, don't. You can't go back there."

Ty took two steps toward her, trying to close the gap between them. But Van countered by scrambling backward, several quick, stuttering steps that were more emotion fueled than finesse.

He held out his hands, like he would with a riled dog. "I have to, Van. You knew I was going back."

"No. You can't."

Tears hit her eyes, making them glisten in the half darkness. They were wide and clear, gorgeous and broken. Ty wanted nothing more than to wrap her in his arms and promise everything was going to be fine.

And he started to say the words. But the flash of memory, Ryan's broken body, had him swallowing them back. His buddy had been laughing, secure in the knowledge that they were in no danger.

War zones held no promises.

"Van."

He called her name. She heard so much yearning in that single word. She wanted it all. More. And he was going to take it all away from her.

She'd known, the minute Ryan came home, a huge grin on his face, so proud that he'd joined the army along with his best friend; Van had known.

A cold rush of grief had washed over her.

She'd known then, at sixteen, that the military would take Ryan's life.

Just as she knew right now, standing in the little log cabin, that if Ty left he'd never come back.

She'd been telling herself for days not to get in too deep. Not to let herself feel or care.

That was impossible.

In a few brief seconds, Van's gaze roamed across Ty's face, down his body and back to the gorgeous gray-blue eyes that haunted her dreams.

She couldn't take it. She couldn't stand to lose him, too.

"Don't go. Please. I'm begging you. Stay. There has to be a way. If you go…" The words clogged in her throat, but she had to find a way to push them out. To make him understand. "You won't come back."

Ty moved closer, crowding into her personal space, but not actually touching her. Neck bent, he stared down at her with that intense, slightly haunted expression he always carried. It was as much a part of him as his blue eyes and the ink that covered his skin. But she couldn't take it. Not right now.

Van turned her head away, staring out the window at the beautiful night. How could the distant mountains and the sliver of silver-black sky be so gorgeous when her body felt ready to crumble in on itself?

"Don't do this, Van," Ty whispered. "Don't do this to yourself. I'll be fine."

Panic welled up from deep inside, a rotten sludge that invaded everything, too powerful to ignore or combat. "No, you won't. I fight death every day, Ty. And most of the time I win. But I wasn't there when Ryan needed me. I won't be there when you need me…and neither will Ryan. We both know he was your voice of reason. You're wild and love to ride the edge of danger. You get off on it."

Ty made a sound deep in his throat, but Van ignored

him. What she was saying was too important. She needed him to *hear*.

"You've always been that way. It's breathtaking and terrifying all at once. I've watched you my entire life. You're fearless and I envy you that inhibition. That ability to look at a situation and not see the potential for pain and suffering the way I do, but rather see it as an obstacle to overcome. A challenge that you can conquer.

"The way you view the world is even more of a gift because your childhood should have taught you to be afraid. To be cautious and careful. But you can't win every time. You've been lucky your entire life. Even when everything went to shit, you always found a way out—"

"So trust that I'll be able to do that again."

She shook her head. Her eyes stung, her nose tingled. But she refused to let the tears win. She would not show a moment of weakness when she needed to be her strongest.

"I can't. Do you know why I work in the ER?"

"Because you're a brilliant doctor and you get the chance to save lives."

"I could do that as a surgeon. As a cardiologist. Hell, more often than not my job requires me to deal with idiots and crazies. But every once in a while, I do get to save a life, which makes the weird and frustrating aspects of the job totally worth it.

"But most of all, I work in the ER because I don't have to care. Not really. Not for long. The patient gets rushed into my trauma room and I jump into action. It's me and my instincts and training against a foe that I refuse to let win. And when I succeed, I send the patient on their way. I don't have to learn their life history. I don't have to spend countless hours with their family."

"You don't have to invest."

"Exactly. And I like it that way because when the worst happens, I don't have to feel the pain down in my bones."

Ty moved closer. One hand settled on her hip, the other wrapped around the curve of her neck, his thumb slipping rhythmically across the base of her throat.

He was so close. So tempting. She could feel the heat of him. His scent surrounded her. It would be so easy to just…give in. To let herself melt against him and let his soothing touch take away all the fear and anxiety.

But it would only last a few minutes, and when the moment was over he'd still be out the door.

And she'd be alone.

"How's that working out for you?"

"Pretty good, actually. Or it was until you swooped back into my life."

She wanted to touch him, but knew that was a bad idea. So, Van let her arms hang loosely at her sides, curling her fingers into her palm in an attempt to keep them from wrapping into his chest and pulling him near.

"Van," he whispered, dipping closer so he could touch his lips to hers.

Turning her head, she let his mouth glance off her jaw instead. "If you walk out that door that's the end of this."

The words physically hurt. They felt like pushing broken glass through her parched throat. But they had to be said.

"I can't be left with no one in my bed and a yard full of dogs to remind me, Ty. I won't. And if you care anything for me at all, you won't ask me to do that."

Ty's forehead pressed against her throat. She heard his harsh breathing, felt the erratic puffs of air slamming against her skin. His body was tense, a solid wall pressed tight against her.

And then it wasn't. All the tension just…slipped away. And for a brief moment she thought maybe she'd won. That he'd heard what she'd said and understood.

As much as there was a part of her that hated herself for making that ultimatum, she knew there was no way she could survive if he left again. Living each day on the edge of disaster, waiting for that visit when someone would tell her that her world had been blown apart a second time.

She was selfish. But if that selfishness saved his life it would be worth it.

Ty stepped back. His movements were reluctant and slow, but the moment she caught the expression on his face, her moment of relief vanished.

His face was a blank canvas. She couldn't read anything there, and that made a trill of panic race down her spine.

"How quickly can you be ready to go? I'll arrange a flight for you and Kaia to get home. Can your parents pick you up in San Antonio? Or do you want me to arrange for a car?"

The pain that lanced through her was so sharp Van was certain she had to be bleeding. Every breath hurt, until the best she could do was pull in quick, shallow draws of air. Not nearly enough.

He was leaving.

And there was nothing more she could do or say to stop him.

16

THE RIDE TO the airport was interminable. Several times, Van almost went back on her ultimatum. But each time she started, Kaia would make a sound or move and she would be reminded all over again what was at stake.

She was weak, but she couldn't live the life Ty needed her to.

They'd had an amazing few days. And that was the extent of what they'd share.

He was quiet and stoic. He didn't even try to kiss her. He simply checked her and Kaia into their flight, handed her the boarding passes and left her outside the security checkpoint.

He didn't even look back.

That, more than anything, had really hurt.

The minute Van got back, she threw herself into work. Staying late, arriving early. Barking orders and generally deteriorating into a foul mood.

Her parents were spending more time with Kaia than she was, but every time she came home and curled up with the dog another fresh wave of grief would take over.

The only time she could escape was when she was elbows deep into work.

A few days slipped into a week. She was bleary-eyed

and exhausted, but unable to stop pushing herself...or her team.

"What the hell were you thinking?" she hollered at the resident currently trying to disappear into the wall behind her. "Do you realize your carelessness could have cost that man his life?"

"I—" The poor girl's words were cut off before she'd barely begun to explain.

"There are no excuses. Mixing these medications could have disastrous results. This is something you should know as a second-year resident. Where's your head, Abby? You're better than this."

"I didn't pull that out, Dr. Cantrell. You did," she finally managed to whisper against Van's tirade.

What the hell was she talking about?

A harsh hand wrapped around her arm, jerking Van sideways. She spun to face whoever was trying to manhandle her only to realize the entire staff had stopped what they were doing and were staring at her in sympathetic disbelief.

And Tina was scowling at her, eyes flashing and pissed.

"Come with me, Dr. Cantrell."

This wasn't her friend talking, it was her boss. The tone of voice made it clear she didn't have a choice in the matter.

Sweeping a hard glance over the staff, Van waited for them to get back to work, then let out a sigh. Some of the anger roiling off Tina vanished, replaced by sympathy tinged with irritation.

Her hold loosened as she guided Van down the hallway and into her office.

Instead of settling behind the desk at the far end of

the room, Tina led them to a pair of armchairs tucked close to the window.

It was bright outside, sunlight streaming through the windows. Van realized she didn't even know what day it was, let alone what time.

Shit, how long had she been here?

"It goes without saying that you're going to take some time off."

"I just did that."

"And apparently it didn't do the trick. Instead of coming back relaxed, you came back wound tighter than a spring ready to blow. I kept hoping that whatever had you spun up would resolve itself, but it's obvious that's not going to happen. So why don't you tell me what happened while you were away? What happened to the guy who was in here? The one you were gaga over."

"I was not gaga over him."

A soft burst of laughter erupted from Tina's mouth.

"Please. It was the talk of the ER for days. No one had ever seen you like that. You wouldn't leave his side. It was obvious he was important to you. Who was he?"

"No one."

Tina shook her head. "Fine. If you don't want to talk to me about it, I'm going to have to require you speak to the staff counselor before I let you back on duty."

"What?" Van jumped to her feet, anger and disbelief flushing her skin a deep red.

Tina just calmly stared up at her. "Sit down, Van. You just erroneously screamed at a resident for a mistake that could have cost a patient his life. You weren't wrong about the mistake, just who was responsible. Luckily, the mix-up was caught. But that doesn't change the fact that you're clearly distracted and upset, and it's affecting your ability to do your job. That's not like you. You're one of the best doctors I have on staff. So, please. Sit down."

Gritting her teeth, Van did as she was told. What else could she do at this point?

Tina's tone softened and she leaned forward in her chair. "I'm worried about you. You've been riding the team so hard they're starting to grumble. And in all the time you've been on the staff I've never heard one single complaint from anyone about how you treat your team. In fact, everyone wants to work with you because you're so calm and efficient. You let everyone do their jobs without trying to micromanage. You correct mistakes with understanding and an affinity for teaching.

"That history is what's preventing me from writing you up for that display out there with Abby. I know this job can be stressful, but you've never been one to let it get to you that way. So, my only assumption is that whatever's bothering you is coming from outside these walls. You can confide in me. Or you can confide in our counselor, but you will talk to someone, Van, before whatever's going on burns a bridge you can't repair. Or costs someone their life, something I know you'd never forgive yourself for."

Van's jaw snapped shut. Anger boiled in her veins. But Tina simply waited.

And suddenly, the anger was gone, replaced by the pain and grief it had poorly masked.

The tears she hadn't let herself shed since coming home suddenly erupted like a geyser.

Aside from offering her a box of tissue, Tina didn't react. She simply let Van work through the emotions on her own. And when the sobs finally began to subside, she asked in a soft, understanding voice, "Want to talk about it?"

They'd been friends and colleagues for years, were close enough that Tina had invited Van over for a backyard barbecue last summer. But they'd never been spill-your-guts-out friends.

Van realized she didn't have any of those. Well, besides Ty.

At the thought of his name more tears threatened, but she shoved them back.

She wanted that. Wanted girlfriends she could gossip with, meet for drinks now and again, and confide in. When had her life gotten so lonely? When had her goals and her work become a poor substitute for living?

With halting words, peppered with hiccups and a few touch-and-go moments when the tears threatened, she shared the entire story with Tina, including her rocky history with Ty and how she'd blamed him for Ryan's life choices and ultimately his death—at least for a little while.

Tina listened, interjecting with questions and comments here and there. But for the most part, she let Van talk. Words she hadn't even realized were pent up inside, begging to burst free, slid out. Thoughts she hadn't let herself truly form found voice.

And when it was done she felt so much better.

And so much worse.

Because it was clear to her that she'd made a terrible mistake. She'd let the fear of losing Ty, of experiencing that loss and finding herself utterly alone, push him away.

Accomplishing what she dreaded most.

"You love him."

Tina's words weren't a question, but Van answered anyway with a nod of her head and a quiet, "Yes."

Tina's lips twisted into a smile. "We see enough pain and suffering on a daily basis, Van. I don't know about you, but that's taught me to appreciate beauty when I have it in front of me. None of us are guaranteed anything, not even a tomorrow. Also another lesson I've learned working here. Don't let fear paralyze you and rob you of something wonderful. Take it while you have it. Enjoy it when you can. And then cherish the moments you were given if it's ever taken away."

God, she was right. So right.

An overwhelming urge to jump out of the chair and race for the first plane she could catch consumed her. But the restless energy had no outlet because it wasn't like she could chase after Ty into a war zone.

Even if she could get into the country, Van had no clue where Ty was actually stationed.

"I screwed up."

"Mmm" was Tina's only comment.

"I don't even know if he cares about me that way. I told him to leave. And he did."

"Luckily, life is full of second, third and fourth chances. I saw the way that man watched you when he was in here. If I had my guess, he cares about you quite a bit. Besides, does it matter? Even if he doesn't, don't you deserve to know one way or the other?"

She definitely did. Pulling her cell out of the pocket of her lab coat, Van didn't hesitate, knowing if she did she might lose her nerve. She loaded Ty's contact and hit Call.

Elephants began stomping in her belly, churning it up and making her feel queasy. The connection took several seconds, longer than normal, but it finally started ringing. And rang and rang before his voice mail kicked in.

The terse, clipped words were beautiful and precious. At the beep, Van froze. She had no idea what to say to him. So she kept it simple.

"Ty, It's Van. I was wrong. I'm sorry. Please call me."

HE'D HIT THE ground and immediately been pulled into a covert ops mission deep inside Afghanistan.

At the moment, he and another handler were in front of a group of soldiers, sweeping through a deserted village. At least it appeared deserted on the surface, but if you looked hard enough it was obvious people had been there recently.

They were undoubtedly in hiding, which could simply be self-preservation or it might be an indication that something bad was going down.

Ty was betting on the latter.

It was dark, clouds obscuring everything but a few meager stars. They'd come in at night on purpose, taking advantage of the cover. But it made his job more difficult.

Echo ranged ahead of him, quickly nosing through debris, trash and rubble in search of anything that might be designed to harm them.

Everything about the situation had him on high alert. It felt too similar to the night he'd lost Ryan. Premonition prickled down his spine and tightened the muscles spanning his shoulders. The gear strapped to his back was heavy, but he didn't really feel it.

He was too hyperaware, his body flooding with adrenaline.

Something caught Echo's attention. His ears pricked and before Ty could issue a command he was darting down a dark, narrow alley. The dog didn't make a sound, not even a warning yip. He trusted that Ty was with him, because they worked together as a team.

Rushing in after Echo, Ty reseated his weapon against his shoulder, ready to respond to any threat. Up ahead, his frame merely a hazy outline in the dark, Echo growled low in his throat.

Shit.

Ty crouched and raced forward, rounding a small out-cropping of crumbled rock that likely used to be a wall, gun pointed and index finger already beginning to de-press the trigger.

And was met by a little, dirty face.

Jerking the muzzle of his gun sideways, Ty skidded to a halt beside Echo, realizing the dog had stopped making the low rumbling noise.

The child stared up at him with deep brown eyes. His face was filthy, with more dirt showing than skin. His body was unnaturally thin. Ty would guess he might be six or seven, but based on his malnourished appearance could potentially be older.

What bothered him most was that the boy didn't ap-pear to react to having a gun pointed straight in his face. He hadn't blinked, just waited, his gaze moving lethar-gically between man and dog.

From behind him, in a low voice, one of the soldiers on the team asked him what was going on. Before Ty could answer, all hell broke loose.

In seconds, Ty was surrounded by gunfire. Dropping to the ground, Ty returned fire. All around him, other soldiers were doing the same. Through the small alley, he could see into the street they'd just been on, and the other dog handler, Sam, who'd been with him just moments ago.

A flash of blinding fire rolled through the area, followed by a boom that would have knocked him on his ass if he wasn't already there.

God, that explosion.

It felt like déjà vu. Ryan's death all over again. The heat of it. The force of the blast rocking through his chest. Sam standing there one moment and then obscured by smoke and debris the next.

His body was frozen for a split second, grief and fear rolling through him. Van's words replayed in his mind. *If you go...you won't come back.*

While he was here on active duty, he couldn't promise her that prediction wouldn't come true. And she was right. He couldn't ask her to sit at home waiting for another phone call telling her someone she loved was gone, which was why he'd walked away.

It had been hard as hell, but the right thing to do. For her.

Ty heard yelling. Voices. Orders. His team was scrambling to regroup. He needed to help them.

And all he could do was stare at the rising plume of black smoke and think that he didn't want to come home to Van in a flag-draped box.

It wasn't cowardice that had him frozen. It wasn't lack of honor or a reluctance to do his job.

At some point in the last few weeks he'd lost that edge, the one that had always carried him straight into danger instead of away from it. The wild streak that had pushed him through the terrible moments of his childhood. The curiosity and recklessness that had him laughing in the face of danger.

Van had tamed him, and he couldn't say that he was upset about it. Because in doing that, she'd given him herself.

Behind him, Echo shifted, dropping on top of the boy. He grunted, the first sound Ty had heard him make.

"Good boy," Ty praised. "Stay."

Ty had no idea what the boy was doing there. He wasn't about to leave a child alone in the middle of a firefight, but he couldn't stay there, either, not when his friends and fellow soldiers needed the backup.

One thing was certain. He needed to finish this mission so he could get home to Van in one piece. And stay there.

17

IT HAD BEEN over a week since she'd left that message on Ty's phone. And she hadn't heard anything. As each day passed, the manic restlessness that had been fueling her bled into panic, then anger and finally a sadness that dug straight into her soul.

Had she burnt her bridges with Ty? Was he going to ignore her call and refuse to give her a chance to apologize? Or was he injured? The unknown was eating away at her.

She compensated with work, but this time, didn't fling herself into it like she had before. She worked her shifts, kept her head and clamped a tight lid over the emotions that threatened to swamp her.

There was no way she'd let her own toxic sludge spill over everyone else in her life again.

But, she was no longer content to retreat into herself. She called her parents and invited them over for dinner one night, realizing that she couldn't remember the last time she'd done that, just because.

She'd rallied several girlfriends and convinced them to meet her at a local bar. She laughed and had a great time. It was nice to open up and get out of the house.

And some mornings she found herself in the park with Kaia, throwing a ball or Frisbee. She'd even talked to several of her neighbors and learned that there was a big end-of-the-summer barbecue in the works. Apparently, it had happened every year, but somehow she'd missed the flyers and invitations over the years she'd been living there. But this year would be different, assuming she wasn't working.

If nothing else, her time with Ty had taught her that it was past time to open up and let other people in to her life.

Sure, the minute she did, she courted the possibility of getting hurt or losing someone important. But it was worth it.

And while she might be fighting against a constant ache centered right in the middle of her chest, she had hopes that eventually the pain would lessen a little.

However, it was difficult to remember that when the doorbell rang, interrupting the first two hours of a planned ten-hour sleep marathon to be followed by a long shift at the hospital.

She was groggy, grumpy and in no mood to deal with whatever soul was parked on her front porch, repeatedly pressing the damn bell.

"I'm coming," she hollered, grumbling under her breath. "Although I make no promises I won't kill you when I get there."

Kaia trailed behind her as she pulled a thin robe over the shorts and tank she'd struggled into before face-planting in the middle of her pillows.

Her fingers didn't want to work, fumbling with the belt. Eventually, she gave up, letting the sides trail open. Whoever it was deserved to get her exactly the way she came.

Eyes still blurry, she yanked the door open. "What do

you…?" and her words trailed off to nothing when she took in the man standing on her front porch.

God, he was gorgeous. There were dark circles under his eyes, telling her he'd probably slept about as much as she had in the last few weeks. His skin was just a little more bronzed than when he'd left, and there was a jagged cut, several days old and well on the way to healing, across the corner of his forehead trailing into his hairline.

"What happened?" Jerking forward, Van's fingers trailed across the cut, poking at the edges before she even registered what she was doing.

Ty's hands wrapped around her waist and gently eased her back.

"I'm fine. It's nothing."

Van harrumphed, crossing her arms over her chest. "Where have I heard those words before?"

Ty just grinned down at her, his beautiful, sensual mouth ripe and begging to be kissed.

God, she wanted to kiss him all over, just so she could make sure he was really there, standing on her front porch.

"What are you doing here?"

Kaia brushed against her thigh and gave a quick yip. The dog sitting on his haunches behind Ty answered with a short bark, but didn't move.

She hadn't even realized the dog was there until now. She'd had eyes only for Ty.

"And who is this?"

"Kaia and Echo are old friends. He and I have been together for almost nine years. Luckily, the army agreed that it was a decent time for him to retire from active duty and join me at the training center in San Antonio when I move there in a couple months."

Van let his words flow over her, slowly sinking in.

"Training center? San Antonio?"

Another grin flashed across Ty's face. "I'm coming home."

"Wait. What? Why?" Van shook her head. He was doing this because of her. Because of what she'd said. And she didn't want that. Dread and regret mixed in her belly, uncomfortable and accusing, making her feel ill. "No. You can't do that, Ty. I was wrong to freak out the way I did. To ask you to change your life because of me. That wasn't—*isn't*—fair. I love you. Fell in love with the man you are, wild streak, reckless proclivities and all. You're worth the risk. The last few weeks have made me realize that I'd rather have three days with you than three lifetimes without you. Any moments we share are a gift."

She was rambling and needed to stop. Now. Snapping her jaw shut, Van stared up at Ty.

And then melted beneath the burning heat shining back at her.

His hands tightened where they rested on her hips, digging into her skin. It should have been uncomfortable, but wasn't. After weeks without him, she needed to feel him on her, deep inside her, anywhere and anyway he wanted.

"You love me?"

A broken laugh stuttered out of her. "Of course I do. How could I not? You're larger than life, Ty Colson. You challenge me and irritate me and make my body burn. You make the sun shine brighter and bring the stars in closer. You're generous and honorable and so damn sexy. You've been through so much, but refuse to let it beat you. You refuse to let the challenges you've faced define you or limit you."

"I barely passed high school, Van."

"I know." She tossed him an impish grin. "I was there. Do you think that matters to me? Grades and degrees aren't the only markers of intelligence in this world. You have an amazing career. You have a way with dogs that's enchanting to watch. You've found your place in the world, the place you belong. And I can't ask you to give that up, especially not for me."

His body convulsed. His arms wrapped around her, pulling her tight into the warmth of his embrace. He enveloped her, surrounded her. And she melted against him, feeling secure in his arms in a way she'd never felt with anyone else, not even her big brother.

She could feel the tiny tremors rocking him, but didn't understand why.

"What's wrong?"

"Nothing," he whispered, the single word ragged and broken. "No one has ever put me first, Van. Not in my entire life. Not my mom, not the man who was my father. Your parents cared, but I always knew their own children came first—as they should. Even with Ryan, as close as we were. I've never had that. Never truly had family."

"You do now," she whispered, fighting back the mingled tears of joy and pain. She hurt for him, because she could hear the echo of the pain he'd buried, remnants of wounds that dug so deeply. She didn't want that for him, but she couldn't change the past. She could only make sure he had something so much better in the future.

Sucking in a deep breath, Ty cupped her shoulders and pushed her away. Dipping his knees, he brought them face-to-face.

"I'm not just doing this for you, Van. It's time. After what happened to Ryan, my heart isn't in it the same way it was. I can do more good training the next soldiers to be the best handlers they can be. That decision just happens to come with the bonus that I'll be moving home to be with you."

Joy clogged her throat, blocking the words she wanted to pour out.

"Savannah Cantrell, I have probably loved you for years, even when I thought you were a bratty little girl and a total pain in the ass."

Van smacked her hand across his shoulder. "Hey!"

His lips tipped up into a half smile, the playful edge softened by the warm glow penetrating his gaze.

"I need you in my life and always will. I want to come home. To you."

"Always."

Scooping her up, Ty kicked the front door closed, not even caring that they'd just given the neighborhood a front-row seat to their heartfelt reunion.

Kaia and Echo bounded around each other, happy to be reunited, but at that moment, Ty only cared about the woman in his arms.

Finding her mouth, he poured everything he had into the kiss. And without reservation, Van gave it right back.

* * * * *

If you loved this story,
be sure to look for RESCUE ME,
Kira Sinclair's next UNIFORMLY HOT! K-9 title.
In stores December 2016.

COMING NEXT MONTH FROM

HARLEQUIN

Blaze

Available September 20, 2016

#911 HIS TO PROTECT
Uniformly Hot! • by Karen Rock

Lt. Commander Mark Sampson hasn't been the same since he left one of his rescue swimmers in a stormy sea. Too bad the beautiful stranger he just spent the night with is the man's sister...and a Red Cross nurse assigned to his next mission!

#912 HER HALLOWEEN TREAT
Men at Work • by Tiffany Reisz

If the best way to get over someone is to get under someone else, handyman Chris Steffensen is definitely repairing Joey Silvia's broken heart. But is Joey's high school friend a guy she could really fall for?

#913 THE MIGHTY QUINNS: TRISTAN
The Mighty Quinns • by Kate Hoffmann

Lawyer Tristan Quinn poses as a writer to start a charm campaign against the residents of a writer's colony who are staunchly opposed to selling. But his fiercest—and sexiest—opponent, Lily Harrison, isn't buying it. So he'll have to up his offensive from charm...to seduction.

#914 A DANGEROUSLY SEXY SECRET
The Dangerous Bachelors Club • by Stefanie London

Wren Livingston must hide her identity from her to-die-for neighbor, Rhys Glover, while he investigates the crime she's committed. But hiding her attraction to him proves impossible after one particularly intimate night...

YOU CAN FIND MORE INFORMATION ON UPCOMING HARLEQUIN® TITLES, FREE EXCERPTS AND MORE AT WWW.HARLEQUIN.COM.

HBCNM0916

REQUEST YOUR FREE BOOKS!
2 FREE NOVELS PLUS 2 FREE GIFTS!

✦ HARLEQUIN®

Blaze®
red-hot reads!

YES! Please send me 2 FREE Harlequin® Blaze® novels and my 2 FREE gifts (gifts are worth about $10). After receiving them, if I don't wish to receive any more books, I can return the shipping statement marked "cancel." If I don't cancel, I will receive 4 brand-new novels every month and be billed just $4.74 per book in the U.S. or $5.21 per book in Canada. That's a savings of at least 14% off the cover price. It's quite a bargain. Shipping and handling is just 50¢ per book in the U.S. and 75¢ per book in Canada.* I understand that accepting the 2 free books and gifts places me under no obligation to buy anything. I can always return a shipment and cancel at any time. Even if I never buy another book, the two free books and gifts are mine to keep forever.

150/350 HDN GH2D

Name	(PLEASE PRINT)

Address	Apt. #

City	State/Prov.	Zip/Postal Code

Signature (if under 18, a parent or guardian must sign)

Mail to the **Reader Service:**
IN U.S.A.: P.O. Box 1867, Buffalo, NY 14240-1867
IN CANADA: P.O. Box 609, Fort Erie, Ontario L2A 5X3

Want to try two free books from another line?
Call 1-800-873-8635 or visit www.ReaderService.com.

* Terms and prices subject to change without notice. Prices do not include applicable taxes. Sales tax applicable in N.Y. Canadian residents will be charged applicable taxes. Offer not valid in Quebec. This offer is limited to one order per household. Not valid for current subscribers to Harlequin Blaze books. All orders subject to credit approval. Credit or debit balances in a customer's account(s) may be offset by any other outstanding balance owed by or to the customer. Please allow 4 to 6 weeks for delivery. Offer available while quantities last.

Your Privacy—The Reader Service is committed to protecting your privacy. Our Privacy Policy is available online at www.ReaderService.com or upon request from the Reader Service.

We make a portion of our mailing list available to reputable third parties that offer products we believe may interest you. If you prefer that we not exchange your name with third parties, or if you wish to clarify or modify your communication preferences, please visit us at www.ReaderService.com/consumerchoice or write to us at Reader Service Preference Service, P.O. Box 9062, Buffalo, NY 14240-9062. Include your complete name and address.

HBI5

"I'm going to go up and see what he's doing." Joey saw a
large green Ford pickup parked behind the house with the
words *Lost Lake Painting and Contracting* on the side in
black-and-gold letters.

"I'll stay on the line," Kira said. "If you think he's
going to murder you, say, um, 'I'm on the phone with my
best friend, Kira. She's a cop.' And if he's sexy and you
want to bang him, just say, 'Nice weather we're having,
isn't it?'"

"It's the Pacific Northwest. In October. It's forty-eight
degrees out and raining."

"Just say it!"

"Now, go check him out. Try not to get murdered."

Joey crept up the stairs and found they no longer
squeaked like they used to. Someone had replaced the old
stairs with beautiful reclaimed pine from the looks of it.

"Hello?"

"I'm in the master," the male voice answered.

Joey walked down the hallway to a partly open door.

There on a step stool stood a man with dirty-blond hair cut neat and a close-trimmed nearly blond beard. He was concentrating on the wiring above his head. He wore jeans, perfectly fitted, and a red-and-navy flannel shirt, sleeves rolled up to his elbows.

"Hey, Joey," he said. "Good to see you again. How's Hawaii been treating you?"

He turned his head her way and grinned at her. She knew that grin.

Oh, my God, it was Chris.

Chris Steffensen. Dillon's high school best friend. That Chris she wouldn't have trusted to screw in a lightbulb, and now he was wiring up a ceiling fan? And seemed to be doing a very good job of it.

"Did you…did you fix up this whole house?" she asked, rudely ignoring his question.

"Oh, yeah. I'm doing some work for Dillon and Oscar these days. You like what we did with the place?"

He grinned again, a boyish eager grin. She couldn't see anything else in the world because that bright white toothy smile took over his face and her entire field of vision. He was taller than she remembered. Taller and broader. Those shoulders of his…well, there was only one thing to say about that.

Joey hoped Kira was still listening.

"Nice weather we're having, isn't it?"

Don't miss HER HALLOWEEN TREAT by Tiffany Reisz, available October 2016 wherever Harlequin® Blaze® books and ebooks are sold.

www.Harlequin.com

HBEXP0916

Reading Has Its Rewards

Earn **FREE BOOKS!**

Register at **Harlequin My Rewards** and submit your Harlequin purchases from wherever you shop to earn points for free books and other exclusive rewards.

Plus submit your purchases from now till May 30th for a chance to win a $500 Visa Card*.

Visit **HarlequinMyRewards.com** today

MYR16R1

JUST CAN'T GET ENOUGH?

Join our social communities
and talk to us online.

You will have access to the latest
news on upcoming titles and special
promotions, but most importantly,
you can talk to other fans about your
favorite Harlequin reads.

Harlequin.com/Community

Facebook.com/HarlequinBooks

Twitter.com/HarlequinBooks

Pinterest.com/HarlequinBooks

HARLEQUIN®
A *Romance* FOR EVERY MOOD™

Stay up-to-date on all your
romance-reading news with the
Harlequin Shopping Guide,
featuring bestselling authors, exciting new
miniseries, books to watch and more!

The newest issue will be delivered right to you
with our compliments! There are 4 each year.

Signing up is easy.

EMAIL

ShoppingGuide@Harlequin.ca

WRITE TO US

HARLEQUIN BOOKS
Attention: Customer Service Department
P.O. Box 9057, Buffalo, NY 14269-9057

OR PHONE

1-800-873-8635 in the United States
1-888-343-9777 in Canada

Please allow 4-6 weeks for delivery of the first issue by mail.